PUBLIC SCHOOL 309
794 MONROE STREET
BROOKLYN, NEW YORK 11221

# HONEYSUCKLE HOUSE

# Honeysuckle House

ANDREA CHENG

FRONT STREET
*Asheville, North Carolina*

Copyright © 2004 by Andrea Cheng
All rights reserved
Printed in China
Designed by Helen Robinson

*Second printing*

Library of Congress Cataloging-in-Publication Data

Cheng, Andrea.
The honeysuckle house / by Andrea Cheng.— 1st ed.
p. cm.
Summary: An all-American girl with Chinese ancestors and a new
immigrant from China find little in common when they meet in their
fourth grade classroom, but they are both missing their best friends
and soon discover other connections.
ISBN 1-886910-99-5 (alk. paper)
[1. Best friends—Fiction. 2. Friendship—Fiction. 3. Chinese Americans—Fiction. 4. Immigrants—Ohio—Fiction. 5. Moving, House-
hold—Fiction. 6. Cincinnati (Ohio)—Fiction.] I. Title.
PZ7.C5585Ho 2003
[Fic]—dc22
2003023112

*To Ann*

**We sit underneath the honeysuckle bush and brush** each
other's hair. Victoria has that kind of thin blond hair
that mats together. Mine is thick and black and hangs
straight. "You're lucky," she says. "Chinese hair doesn't
tangle."

"It does a little," I say, "but my mom brushes it every
morning."

"She does?" Victoria is always surprised about my
mom. "What's she doing now?" Victoria inhales deeply.

I sniff too. We hear pots and pans and water running.
"Making soup, I think."

"How do you *make* soup?"

"Out of vegetables and water and bones."

"Real bones? Where's she get them?"

"From the grocery store," I say, pulling on a tough
tangle until Victoria hunches her shoulders. "Sorry." I
smooth her hair with my hand.

"Victoria." It's her mother calling.

"Yes, ma'am." She stands up so fast that she jerks

the brush out of my hand. I practically push her out the door of the honeysuckle house, because if she doesn't go home fast enough her mother won't let her play outside again for a whole week. That already happened twice, and without Victoria, a week is a very long time.

I brush my bangs and wait for her to come back out. If I lift my eyebrows I can feel the stiffness of my hair on my forehead. Victoria's two kittens come in and purr and rub against my legs. One rolls over in the dry leaves. The other settles on my lap, and I rub his fuzzy kitten fur. Still no Victoria.

My brother Sam pushes the branches of the doorway apart. "Hey, Sarah, you want to play something?"

"I'm petting the kitty," I say.

"When you're done."

"Play what?"

"Four-square."

"You mean two-square."

"Yeah, two-square."

I sigh. "Okay. Until Victoria comes back out."

Sam tries all sorts of tricks he's picked up on the school playground—pitty-patty, cherry bomb, poison ivy—but still I beat him and move into D. Sweat forms on Sam's forehead, he is trying so hard. I think for a minute of letting him win like I used to when he was little. Right when I'm not paying attention, he puts a baby ball into the corner. "You're out," he says triumphantly.

Mom calls us in for lunch.

"I'm in D after lunch," Sam says.

"If I still want to play."

We have Mom's noodle soup. After lunch, the three of us make a peach pie. Mom mixes up the crust, I cut the peaches, and Sam takes out the pits.

"Dad loves peach pie," Sam says.

"He's in Atlanta," I say.

Mom corrects me. "Saint Louis."

"Same difference."

"I'll save him a piece anyway," Sam says. "Will I be asleep when he gets home?"

Mom nods.

The corners of Sam's mouth turn down. He is always waiting for Dad to come home. He leaves notes for Dad all over the house. *Dear Dad, I missed you today.* Then in big block letters he writes, *LOVE YOUR SON SAM.*

I slice the next peach carefully around the middle and pull the two halves apart. "Perfect," says Sam, taking out the pit. "I'm going to plant this pit and grow a peach tree."

"You can give it a try," Mom says.

"It won't work," I say.

"How do you know?"

"I've tried it."

"They must grow peach trees somehow."

"Go ahead and plant it if you want." That's Sam, doing things even when he knows they won't work. He sets a place for Dad at the table, even when Mom says he probably won't be home until late. "Just in case," he says. Then we have to clear away the empty plate for nothing.

Sam goes out to plant the peach pit. He pokes his head

back in. "Victoria's waiting for you," he says.

I stand up so fast that I knock over the bowl of peaches. Some slide onto the floor. Mom sighs. "What's your hurry?"

"Nothing." I shove the peaches back into the bowl and take a quick swipe at the floor with a sponge before heading out.

"Was the soup good?" Victoria asks as soon as I duck under the branches.

"Yup. You want to try some?"

Victoria wrinkles her nose. "I'm afraid to eat real bones."

"You don't eat them. They're just for flavor."

"I don't like bone flavor." She takes a big sniff. "What's she making now?"

"Peach pie."

"You guys make everything, don't you?"

"Not everything." I notice then that her eyes are red around the edges. "What's wrong?"

Victoria stirs the dirt around with a stick. She's like that. She never tells you right away. "Want to play orphan?" she asks. Her voice is croaky.

It's fun to play orphan but it might make her even sadder. "How about we play Indian," I suggest.

Victoria shakes her head. "Orphan's more fun." The redness is going away a little. "This is our orphanage, and we have to gather food for dinner."

"We can make pokeberry stew." I head out to pull the purple pokeberries off the weeds that are taller than Sam. My fingers turn magenta right away. "We can use the berries to dye our clothes too," I say, watching a magenta spot on my T-shirt spread.

Sam brings us a handful of peach pits. "Do you need some of these?"

"They can be the bones," Victoria says, adding them to the stew.

I pull up a handful of sweet clover. "Herbs," I say. I have an idea. I run into the house to get some string and tie it between two honeysuckle branches. "We better prepare for the harsh winter ahead." I make small bundles of grass and clover to hang from the string.

"It's a clothesline," says Victoria.

"To dry the herbs."

"What are herbs for anyway?"

"Flavor."

"Like the bones?"

"Yup."

"Can I be an orphan too?" Sam asks.

"Are there boy orphans?" I ask Victoria.

"Not usually," she says. "But I guess there could be. Anyway, he can be the brother orphan to keep you company after I'm gone."

"Gone?"

"We're moving."

"Really?" I'm not sure if she is Victoria the neighbor or Victoria the orphan.

"Yup. My mom says."

I'm not sure if I should believe Victoria's mother. She told Victoria that they were going to Disney World and I could go with them, but they never went. She said they were going to plant flowers around their oak tree. She bought hundreds of impatiens, but she never planted them and they shriveled in their small black cartons. But when she said Victoria couldn't play for a week, she wouldn't let her come out even once.

"Where are you moving to?" I ask.

"I don't know." Victoria's eyes get red again and I'm sorry I asked. "Let's pretend we're sisters and we got left on the steps of the orphanage because our parents didn't want us anymore," she says.

"The brother got left too," says Sam.

Victoria starts crying and saying "I want Mommy" in a baby voice. The crying sounds fake, but she has real tears on her cheeks. Sam says, "I miss Daddy, I miss Daddy."

"Stop it, Sam," I say.

"Victoria." Her mother's calling, but Victoria keeps crying and stirring the pokeberries around.

"You better hurry." I hold back the branches of the doorway.

"Your mom's calling you," Sam says.

Victoria still doesn't stop.

"You better go or your mom might not let you come out tomorrow," I remind her.

"I can't come out anyway. We're moving."

"Today?"

Victoria's mother calls again, louder.

"Here, take some stew." Sam pushes a fistful of berries and peach pits toward Victoria.

"She doesn't need that." I push Sam's hand away.

Victoria's mom comes closer. I can see her legs between the branches. I don't think I've ever been so close to her before. Her legs look young and smooth. Mom doesn't like to wear shorts because her legs have purple veins, but Victoria's mom has legs that are all white. "Victoria, come here this instant," she says.

Victoria ducks underneath the branches and walks slowly toward her mother.

Through the honeysuckle branches I watch Victoria carry an armload of clothes out to the car. A pair of shorts falls onto the ground, and when she picks it up she drops a sock. Her mom carries a lamp without a shade. Victoria gets into the back seat with the clothes and the lamp. Her mother is about to start the car. Then she goes back into the house and comes out with one of the kittens and a black dress on a hanger. She hands Victoria the kitten through the open car window and goes around the car to the driver's side. Could they really be about to move? Victoria looks my way. I run out of the honeysuckle house just as the car starts.

"Here, take this." I thrust my hairbrush through the car window.

"Thanks." Victoria lets the brush fall onto the kitten in her lap.

Her mom puts the car into drive and the tires roll over all the small acorns. "You dropped a sock," Sam says, but the car is already partway down the hill. I watch it go around the bend. My eyes get watery and I wonder if they are red around the edges like Victoria's, but I have browner skin. Victoria always says how lucky I am because her white skin lets everything show through.

I should have asked Victoria more, like when they're coming back, but whenever her eyes get red, the only thing to do is pretend something to make the redness go away.

"Want to play two-square now?" Sam asks softly.

I don't say anything, because if I do, I'll start crying. If I go inside, Mom will ask me what's wrong. Sam will tell her that Victoria moved away. Mom will pat my head the way she does Sam's when he misses Dad. She'll explain that Victoria's mom has a lot of problems. She'll say that I'm lucky I have two parents and a brother. But I don't feel like thinking about my good luck. I run my fingers through my hair and a honeysuckle leaf floats to the ground.

Sam and I stay out until it's almost dark, adding more pokeberries and black-eyed-Susan petals to the stew. Sam finds small acorns too. I check every car that goes down the street. Maybe they just took the clothes somewhere. Victoria's cousin lives on the other side of town. Maybe they went there for a few days.

We have my favorite baked chicken and squash for dinner. Since there are only the three of us, we eat at the kitchen table. Sam tells Mom that Victoria moved.

"Really?" Mom raises her eyebrows.

Sam nods. "That's what she said."

Mom looks out the kitchen window at Victoria's house. It's so close to ours you can see everything. Against the wall is a bookcase with a set of encyclopedias standing neatly in a row. In the middle of the room is an exercise bike. "I doubt they really moved. All their things are still in the house."

"But they took some of their stuff," Sam says.

"Their furniture is still there," Mom says. "They need a moving truck."

"Victoria said they were moving," I whisper. Then the lump in my throat swells up so fast I can't swallow. I push my plate of chicken away and run up the stairs to my room. From my bed I can see right into Victoria's room. The light is on by her bed and the window is wide open even though it is October. *The Boxcar Children* is on her pillow. I gave it to her for her last birthday. Sometimes we pretend that the honeysuckle house is our boxcar. We manage to survive on our own like Henry and Jesse and Violet and Benny. Then we forget about Victoria's mom who keeps her inside for a whole week and my dad who is in Chicago or Atlanta or Saint Louis while Sam and Mom are waiting.

Mom is coming up the stairs. She turns in at my door. I cover my head with my pillow. Why did Sam have to say anything about Victoria moving? He can never keep his mouth shut. Mom will tell me that I'll make new friends. She's not too happy about Victoria living right next door anyway. Their house is getting all run down. The shades are torn. A big piece of stucco fell off the side. I've never been inside her house, but Victoria said the kitchen cabinets were on the floor because they were going to get new ones but never did. Last week Mom and another neighbor were talking about what an eyesore the house has become.

I know Mom is standing in the doorway, but when I don't sit up she goes back downstairs. I take the pillow off my head and the air in my room feels so cold. The headlights of a car move slowly across the wall. I cup my hands around my face and look out. It's not Victoria or Dad.

I toss and turn in my bed. Without my quilt I feel cold, but with it I'm sweaty. The light from Victoria's lamp makes my room too bright. I push my window farther open and move my head to the other side of the bed. The air is so warm, it feels like summer instead of fall. A squeaking sound comes through the window. I sit up and cup my hands around my eyes. The kitten that was left behind is meowing in our side yard.

I tiptoe into the hallway and call downstairs. "Mom?"

"Why aren't you asleep?" Mom is irritated. She's strict about bedtime on school nights.

"The other kitten is out there."

"The other kitten?"

"The one Victoria didn't take."

The kitten is sitting by the screen door. Mom sighs. "Take a bowl of milk out to the porch."

The kitten purrs and rubs against my leg. Its tiny tongue laps at the milk. "Don't worry," I tell him, "your brother will be back soon." I fold a towel in half and put it on the chair. "Here's your bed, kitty." The kitten jumps up on the towel and stares at me.

On my way back to my room, I stop in Sam's doorway for a minute. He lifts his head.

"Dad?"

"Dad's not home yet."

Sam turns his head toward the wall.

"He'll be home soon."

Sam doesn't turn my way.

"Hey, Sam."

"What?" His voice is muffled.

"Tomorrow we can play two-square."

Sam doesn't answer. I feel bad that he never got to be in D. I feel bad that I can't make him stop missing Dad. I wait for a few minutes, but he won't turn back around.

Victoria is absent from school all week. "Sarah, do you know anything about Victoria?" Miss Renfro asks on Friday. "I've called her house several times, but nobody answers."

"They left on Sunday," I say.

Miss Renfro raises her eyebrows. "Left?"

I nod.

"I see," she says, making a mark in her grade book.

The girl next to me, Naomi, pokes me with her elbow. "Where'd she go?"

I shrug.

"Her mom's pretty strange," Naomi says. "Remember that time she came to school?" She giggles.

For some reason I want to defend Victoria's mom. "I don't remember," I say, even though I do. Victoria's mom brought Hostess cupcakes to our classroom last year for Victoria's ninth birthday. She was wearing a mini-skirt and a shirt with silver sequins. She laughed so loud you could hear it even in the bathroom. Victoria wouldn't look at her mother. She wouldn't take a single bite of the cupcake. I told Victoria they were the best cupcakes I ever had. Then I ate hers so her mom wouldn't know she didn't even try her own birthday cupcakes.

Miss Renfro is talking about a new girl who has just come from China. My stomach tightens. I'll have to tell everyone all over again that I don't speak Chinese. Why couldn't the new girl join the other fourth-grade class? Their class is smaller than ours. Is it because I am Chinese that they picked Miss Renfro's? I run my hand through my tangled hair. Mom wanted to brush it this morning, but I jerked my head away. It was just fine, I told her, just fine the way it was.

The principal brings the new girl right to Miss Renfro's desk. She has the two neatest ponytails I've ever seen and a perfectly straight part. Each ponytail has three colored rubber bands. "This is Tina," Miss Renfro says.

"Looks just like you," the boy behind me whispers. "Is she your cousin?"

The blood rushes to my face.

Miss Renfro scans the class and then turns to Tina. "There's an empty seat next to Sarah. She'll help you get started." Miss Renfro points to Victoria's empty desk, but Tina doesn't move. "Sarah, come and show Tina her new seat."

I stand up slowly and make my way to Miss Renfro's desk. Tina follows me back to the seat. The class is so quiet you can hear Tina's hard shoe soles on the floor. Everyone is watching. *Sisters*, they are thinking. Maybe

I should tell everyone that Tina is my long-lost twin from China. I know they'll believe it. In first grade, an Asian girl named Emma was in our class. The art teacher called me Emma the whole year. Mom said I should say, "Excuse me, Miss Clark, my name is Sarah," but whenever it happened, I got sweaty and I knew my voice would come out croaky.

Miss Renfro tells us to take out our journals. Tina watches me and takes a small notebook out of her Lucky Dog book bag. She opens to the first page and writes *Tina Liang* in perfect handwriting on the light graph paper. I look at my blank paper. Usually journal writing is my favorite time of the day. I write fast and furiously with arrows all over the page. Miss Renfro loves my stories. Sometimes she writes *Fantastic* in red ink on the top of the page. Victoria likes my stories too. I read them out loud to her in the honeysuckle house. If the story isn't finished, we think of the next chapter. We added so many chapters to the story about the kids on the island that it filled up the whole notebook. We couldn't think of a good title, so Victoria wrote *The Novel* in curly handwriting on the cover. Under that she drew a map of an island with palm trees and sandy beaches. When we were finished, Victoria took the novel into her house so she could show it to her mom.

Tina hunches over her paper and writes a paragraph with no cross-outs at all. Her handwriting is small and perfect. Finally I write two sentences, one about fall leaves and one about buckeyes.

At recess, Tina stands right by me on the playground. "Can she talk?" Naomi asks.

"I don't know," I say. "She wrote a whole paragraph in her journal."

"Say something to her in Chinese," a boy says.

"I don't speak it."

"You must know something."

"I don't."

Soon a whole group of kids is standing around us, trying to get Tina to talk. "Speak English?" Naomi asks.

Tina looks down. She has tears coming out of her eyes, but she doesn't make any sound at all. Most of the kids back off when they see her crying. She holds on to the chain-link fence and watches the cars on the road. Maybe she really does want to be alone. Sometimes I want to be alone too. I look at Tina's face streaked with tears. The cars are speeding by. I see a maroon Toyota, but it goes by so fast I can't tell if there is a white-haired girl in the back seat. "Maybe that was my friend," I say, pointing at the car just before it rounds the bend. "She moved away."

"My friend in China," Tina says.

# T I N G

●

**When Ma Ma left Shanghai for America, I didn't know**
it would be so long before I saw her again that I forgot
her smell. Not quite, but when I did finally see her, more
than one year had passed and her smell had changed.
There was no more of her soft perfume along with the
anise that she put in the soup. Ma Ma had a sharp soap
smell instead. It was so strange to me that I almost didn't
recognize her.

The flight attendant brought me to her. I'd been asleep
on the plane so my careful pigtails were all messed up.
At first I wasn't even sure that it really was Ma Ma, and
I held tightly to the hand of the lady. Grandma Po Po
had asked her to deliver me safely to my mother. I wasn't
scared. When Po Po told me to be brave on the long trip,
I wondered why she said that. Sitting on a plane with a
nice lady to watch over me wasn't scary. But now when I
smelled the sharp soap, I knew what she meant.

"Ting, you have grown so tall," Ma Ma said, scooping
me into her arms. The lady left and tears came out of my

eyes. "Don't cry, Ting," Ma Ma said, wiping my face with her palm. "We'll go home and have some soup. Noodle soup to celebrate that you are in America." I listened to Ma Ma's words. Her voice was the same as I remembered it.

"Where is Ba Ba?" I asked.

"He had to go to Chicago. He'll come back to see you very soon."

I tried to imagine how my father looked, but all I could remember was the smoky smell of his clothes. I held tightly to Ma Ma's hand as we went through the airport. The voices around us were so flat. No up and down sounds. When I was in Shanghai, Uncle said I should learn English. He found an English teacher who came to our apartment every Wednesday and Friday after school. She had ten English books and I finished all of them. But at the airport, I didn't hear the words in my books.

I gripped Ma Ma's hand, so much smoother than Po Po's.

The noodle soup was almost the same but not quite. In my mouth it was fine, but the smell was not right. I had only a few spoonfuls.

"You don't like soup anymore? Now you like meat?"

I shook my head. The room was spinning. The kitchen stove was gigantic. It even had a door like a room.

"What's that?" I asked.

"Oven," Ma Ma said in English. She explained in Chinese. "It gets very hot inside." In Shanghai, we didn't have an oven. Po Po cooked everything on an electric hot plate on the landing. Soup, noodles, everything. Ma Ma showed me my bed. It had a blue plaid blanket on it. The room was like a closet with a small window at the end.

"Can I sleep with you?" I asked. In China I slept with my cousin Hong. She took all the covers and pushed me into a small space against the wall, but still I was not alone.

"In America you have your own room," Ma Ma said.

The bed was so fresh and new. My nightgown had the same soapy smell as the noodles. The air was too quiet. In Shanghai when I went to bed I heard Uncle slurping soup and Po Po washing dishes in the bathroom sink and Mr. Liu from across the street shouting to his brother. Then I heard Uncle take his carving tools out of his desk drawer. Sometimes he let me watch him carve the small stone stamps. His hands were steady and sure as he carved a single Chinese character on the end of the stone stick. Sometimes he carved a monkey or a rabbit just for me. But here in America, there were no sounds. When we'd come into the apartment, we passed four doors. Ma Ma said other people lived there, but they were very quiet people.

I stood on my bed and looked out the window. There were trees and bushes and a dumpster. In China, it was thirteen hours ahead. Maybe Po Po and Uncle and Hong were having lunch. Hong was happy because she could have more soup for herself. Po Po always told her she shouldn't be so greedy, but still, when nobody was watching, she took the fish cheek all for herself. Maybe she was happy now that I was gone and she wouldn't have to hide what she ate.

After "oven," the next new word I learned in English was "green card." It seemed that this green card was very important. When I asked Ma Ma, she said that Ba Ba had gone to Chicago to see about getting this green card from a place called Immigration. Without it, he could not get a job. It would be against the law and he could be locked up in jail or sent back to China. Ba Ba might have to stay in Chicago for a while. Maybe we would go too. Ma Ma wasn't sure. For now we would stay in Cincinnati where she had a job cleaning four houses and a school close by where she could study English. Soon I would start fourth grade.

"What is my new school called?" I asked.

"Pleasant Hill School," she said.

I said the name over and over. It sounded like a nice school.

"When does school start?" I asked.

"It has already started. That's okay. The lady said you could start whenever you arrived."

I drew a picture of my school in Shanghai right by the bicycle shop. Then I drew another picture of a small red school on top of a big hill. I put children on the hillside and flowers too. When Ma Ma finished washing the dishes, we walked to my new school.

"Where are all the people?" I asked.

"America is not crowded like Shanghai," Ma Ma explained.

There were lots of trees with leaves just starting to turn orange. The school had a nice big tree right in front. Maybe I could climb it someday. On the door of the school building was a big painted frog.

"I like frog," I said, remembering Po Po's frog soup.

"In America we don't eat frog," Ma Ma said. "Don't say anything about eating frog at school."

Maybe in America everything I said would be wrong.

We went right to the office. The secretary smiled at us and went to get the principal. He smiled too. Ma Ma translated his words for me. I would be in Room 102. He gave me a name tag that said *Tina*. This would be my American name. I would need school supplies before I could start school. Miss Renfro, my new teacher, would be waiting for me tomorrow morning.

Ma Ma wrote *Tina Liang* on my notebook and jacket and book bag. She gave me a sharp pencil and told me to practice my new English name. In Chinese, my name was only two characters, but in English it had nine letters. I wrote it on the paper five times until it was perfect. I practiced saying *Tina Liang* until it rolled off my tongue. Ma Ma said I was a smart girl. I told her I already knew how to write whole paragraphs. Then Ma Ma wrote my address and told me to copy it until I knew it by heart: *3828 Whitaker Street, Apartment 4, Cincinnati, Ohio 45229*. Ma Ma wrote a letter to Po Po and Uncle telling them that I was such a good, sweet girl and I already knew so much English. She thanked Uncle for hiring such a good English teacher. She also wrote that Ba Ba was still in Chicago because of the green card.

At the end of Ma Ma's letter I wrote *Tina Liang* so that Po Po and Uncle could see my new name. When our letter was done, Ma Ma told me to walk down to the mailbox and drop the letter in.

Still I saw no people. There was nobody but me. A dog tied to a tree wagged its tail, but I didn't dare go closer. I pulled the handle at the top of the mailbox and dropped the letter in. Without it in my hand, I felt even more alone. Why did people in America stay inside? I passed an apartment house like ours. A curtain opened and I saw a girl's face, but then it was gone.

When I got home, Ma Ma told me to play out back and get some fresh air. I passed the four apartment doors again. In Shanghai, I went to Mrs. Tang's apartment anytime. I played airplane with her little grandson. The door was always open.

The sun was hot on my back, so I went into the shade of the dumpster. I drew lines in the dirt like airplane lines. Maybe the plane I came on left a white line in the sky. When Hong and Uncle and Po Po looked up, they saw the white line from my airplane in the sky. Hong would say she was glad I was gone. Po Po would tell her not to say things like that. Maybe at recess Mu Ying would see the white line too. She would think, *My best friend Ting is on that airplane.*

I climbed into a mulberry tree that was growing by the dumpster and looked down at my lines. They crisscrossed, forming squares and rectangles. I swung down from a branch like a monkey in the jungle. My very own jungle. A plant had sprouted underneath the tree. It would die in the shade. Po Po was always moving her plants from one window to another in the tiny apartment to catch the rays of the sun. What could I use to dig a hole? Maybe there was something in the dumpster. I climbed up the side and looked down. A metal spoon stuck out of a bag. I swung myself down into the dumpster. Bees were all around. Hong hated bees, but I wasn't scared. The dumpster smelled worse than the fish market in Shanghai. The sides were steep. What if I couldn't get out? Footsteps came closer. Someone threw a bag of garbage over the edge, and it landed by my feet. I put the metal spoon in my pocket and gripped the top edge of the dumpster with my fingers. I was good at climbing. Hong said I really was a monkey. My feet slipped for a minute, but then I was over the top.

I dug a hole in the sun and transplanted the small plant. Maybe it would grow into a big tree like the one in front of the school.

"Ting, where are you?" Ma Ma called.

"Over here," I said, moving in front of the dumpster.

Ma Ma brushed off my shirt. "You got dirty already," she said. Po Po didn't like it either when I got dirty. She said Hong never got as dirty as I did. "Better come in and take a bath," Ma Ma said. "You have to get ready for your first day of school tomorrow."

Ma Ma told me to not be scared and to show the world how good Chinese children were. I nodded. Anyway, there was nothing to be afraid of. I was Tina Liang with a real American name and I knew English.

The teacher asked another Chinese girl named Sarah to take care of me. Right away Sarah said, "I don't speak Chinese." At recess I followed her onto the playground. She took big steps like she wanted to get ahead of me. If Mu Ying had been there, she would take small steps. All the other kids were running in different directions across the field. I hurried to catch up with Sarah.

After recess my teacher took me to another room that only had eight kids. Some were older than me and some were younger. I thought one boy might be from China, but when I told him in Chinese that my name was Liang Ting he looked away. The teacher gave me a sheet with the alphabet to copy. I did it perfectly, it was so easy. Why didn't she give me real work to do? She drew a smiling face on my paper, but I didn't feel like smiling. I put my head down on the table and stayed like that until school was over and I could run to Ma Ma.

I told Ma Ma that I wanted to go back to Shanghai.

"Oh, Ting, you'll get used to school. This is just the first day. Uncle will be so proud when we write him that you are speaking English already."

I wanted to tell Ma Ma that I barely said a word all day, but I kept my face blank. Then I said, "I want to go back to my own school with Mu Ying."

Ma Ma's face got stern. "No, Ting. Here in America there is opportunity."

"What is opportunity?"

"Opportunity is very important."

"For what?"

"You will see, Ting."

The next day I listened carefully to the teacher, Miss Renfro, and the kids. I would learn English perfectly so nobody would even know that I came from China. Then I could laugh and joke with all the girls. Like Sarah. She had a Chinese face, but English words were in her mouth.

I watched her lips and her tongue. At home I would practice in front of the mirror, pushing the air softly so my words would stay flat. Sarah's words were slow and careful, and she waited until my sentences stumbled out of my mouth. She told me about her little brother Sam.

"That's him over there."

I could see because he was the only Chinese boy. "He is very cute," I said.

"Do you have any sisters or brothers?" Sarah asked.

I shook my head. "No brother no sister. I have my cousin and I have my friend Mu Ying."

Other girls tried to listen to us, but their big round eyes were scary. My eyes got watery. The girls stared at my hair. Was my part crooked? I felt my long pigtails. Ma Ma had put three rubber bands on each one to make sure they stayed neat. Tomorrow I would wear my hair without the extra rubber bands like the other girls.

## SARAH

**Victoria hasn't come back for over a month. I want to** go out on my bicycle to look for her, but both tires are flat and I can't find the pump. Sam says the tires won't hold air anyway. He already tried pumping them up. I sit on the seat and balance for a minute without pedaling. There's no way I can ride all over the city on flat tires.

Maybe they moved far, like way out in Indiana. When we drove to Chicago there were cornfields all around us for miles and miles. Maybe Victoria moved to a farm like that in the middle of a cornfield. She said that someday she was going to have a horse. I told her she was lucky because at least she has two kittens. Mom won't let us have any pets. She says two kids are more than enough to take care of, especially since Dad's always out of town. Once when Dad came back from Tampa, he brought us a goldfish in a bowl. The next day it was floating on top of the water. Sam wanted to bury the fish, but it was winter so we just flushed it down the toilet. Sam wouldn't stop crying. Mom looked at Dad and said "See?" even though it wasn't Dad who killed the fish.

I sit on the concrete steps out front and look over at Victoria's. A tiny oak tree has sprouted in the gutter. A squirrel runs along the edge of the roof and disappears under the eaves. Maybe it's making a nest in Victoria's house.

The kitten walks around me, rubbing on my sweat-shirt. Its fur is getting thicker and darker. Even though Mom says the kitten isn't really ours, she bought a small bag of cat food that we keep on the porch. Sam wants to name the kitty McKenzie, but I tell him it's Victoria's kitty and she'll name it whatever she wants. She just hasn't decided yet. Sam is bouncing a playground ball.

"Want to play?" he asks.

I shake my head.

"I never got to be in D, remember?"

I remember, but I don't feel like playing. "Not right now."

Sam's skinny shoulder blades stick out as he dribbles. Mom comes out and sits down next to me on the steps. She runs her fingers through my hair. It's all tangled. This morning I told Mom that I would brush it out myself with the new brush she bought to replace the one I gave to Victoria, but the bristles scratched my scalp. I did only the bangs.

"Sarah, maybe you should cut your hair if you don't want to brush it," Mom says. Sam's hair flies up as he reaches for the ball. I touch the back of my head where my hair is matted.

"I want it cut short."

"Really?" Mom is surprised. Usually I resist even a trim.

"I'll get the scissors," I say.

Mom starts in front by my ears and goes around. Little bits of hair fall onto the concrete steps.

When she's done, I feel the back. "Can you cut it shorter?"

"Are you sure? It'll take a while to grow back."

The tangles are still there. Whenever I brush my hair, I miss Victoria even more. Long hair is just a big bother. I think of Tina's perfect pigtails. I wonder if her scalp gets sore from the tight rubber bands. If my hair is short, nobody will think we look alike. "I'm sure," I say.

The scissors come close to my ear. Big clumps of hair land on the steps and on my lap. The kitty bats them with his small paws. Mom takes a long time to get the layers just right. My neck is stiff from sitting still.

"Okay," Mom says, "it's done."

My head is so light when I shake it. Suddenly I feel like I am sitting in my front yard without a shirt.

"Hey, now we look alike," Sam says. "Like twins." He touches my head.

"Yup," I say, trying to sound cheerful. "But people already think I have a twin."

"Who's that?" Mom asks.

"The new girl, Tina."

Sam scrunches up his face. "That girl with the pony-tails?"

I nod.

"Well, they won't mix you two up anymore," Sam says.

What will Victoria say when she sees me? How will we brush each other's hair when mine is so short? The kitty is batting clumps of my hair underneath the bush. I wish I could reattach it, tape it back together.

We go with Mom to buy groceries. When I see my reflection in the front window, I almost go back to the car. I look strange, like I need a hat to cover my head. I look like a boy. What would it be like if I really were a boy? Dad would play football with me the way he does with Sam. He would call me "son." Dad would be so happy to have another boy like Sam. But I might be a different kind of boy, one who spills things and trips over the steps.

A lady goes by with a cart full of chips and Coke. A girl follows along with a head of hair so white it glows. I suck in my breath. Her back is to us. Her legs are thin. Her hair is matted. I walk across the aisle to see her face. Brown far-apart eyes. The girl stares at me and I automatically put my hand to my hair. The short ends are bristly on my fingers.

Everyone in the store is looking at me. Maybe Mom cut the back too short. I decide to wait for Mom and Sam in the car. People push carts past me. A small boy is eating a Pop-Tart. I wish I had a book. I wish I'd stayed home.

We stop at the plant store to get flower bulbs. I scan the kids playing on the swings over by the greenhouse. No white hair. Sam asks me to push him even though he knows how to pump, so I get him started. Victoria loves swings. Once Mom took Victoria and Sam and me to a park with a big tire swing. I was afraid to go real high, but not Victoria. Push me higher, she kept telling me, higher. The sun came from behind and lit up her head when she was in the sky. From there, she could see the Ohio River, she said. When we got home, the honeysuckle house was our houseboat on the river, and our parents were fishermen. We caught fish in big nets that we hauled over the edge of our boat. Sam jumps off the swing in midair and lands right on his feet.

"Should we get yellow daffodils or yellow and white ones?" Mom asks.

"How about both?" I suggest.

Mom is reading the directions that come with the bulbs. Dad used to take care of the yard, but now that Mom isn't working, she cuts the grass and weeds the flower bed. "We better get some bone meal too," Mom says.

"What for?"

"It's like food for the bulbs," Mom says.

"Is it really made of bones?" Sam asks.

"I guess so."

"What kind?"

"Any kind," I say. I am in a hurry to get home.

We pick out thirty bulbs, fifteen yellow and fifteen mixed. Some bulbs have baby ones attached. Mom says you have to divide them every year so they don't get too crowded, and add more of the bone meal. She's been taking gardening books out of the library so she knows what to do. Whenever Mom's stuck on something, she goes to the library. Books are a wealth of information, she says. The other day she borrowed a book about teenagers even though I'm only ten. The cover had a girl with tight jeans and mean eyes glaring at her mother. I didn't even want to open that book because of the mean girl.

While Mom is paying for our bulbs, Sam wants to swing again. "Come on, Sarah," he says. His skinny legs are pumping fast and his black hair is flying. I take the swing next to him and soon we are swinging exactly at the same time, so high I feel the swing set pop.

"Hey, sonny, slow down," a man says. He is looking right at me. I feel the blood rush to my face. Now everyone thinks I am a boy. I should tell him, "I'm a girl, sir." I should have told Miss Clark my name was Sarah, not Emma. I stop pumping and my swing slows down. "That's more like it," the man says.

Mom digs holes underneath our elm tree with a small trowel. Sam puts the bulbs in. I sprinkle on the bone meal and cover them up with dirt. The squirrels watch from Victoria's roof.

"Let's not tell Dad we planted them," Sam says. "It can be a surprise." Then he asks Mom when Dad's coming home.

"Soon," Mom says. "If he made the connection in Atlanta."

"And if he misses it, when's he coming?"

"About four in the morning."

I see Sam cross his fingers. Not me. I used to be like Sam and Mom and wait for Dad to come home. He brought us souvenirs from every city—key chains with baseballs and arches, socks with skyscrapers. But then he missed so many planes. The meetings ran over. He had to stay overnight in Baltimore or Minneapolis.

"Sarah. You're forgetting about the bone meal."

I pour some in. "Sorry."

The kitty paws at the hole. "Stop it, McKenzie," Sam says.

"I told you, that's not his name."

"To me it is," Sam says.

"He's not even ours, so how can we name him?"

"Victoria just called him 'kitty,' and that's not a name. How would you like to be named 'person'?"

"Fine by me."

"Stop bickering," Mom says.

She goes in to fix dinner and Sam and I plant the rest of the bulbs ourselves. There are six left over in the bag when all of Mom's holes are filled. "How about we plant them around the orphan house?" Sam says.

Digging the holes is harder than I thought. The trowel bends when I push too hard. Finally I make six holes in a semicircle around the entrance. Sam puts the bulbs in, adds the bone meal, and covers them up. Together we pat the soil firmly over the top. When we are done, I crawl inside the honeysuckle house to see how things are. Sam follows me. The bunches of herbs have fallen off, but the string is still there. Pokeberries from our stew are shriveled on the stone seats. Curly oak leaves have blown all around the hearth. I sweep them into a pile with my hands.

"It'll be pretty with the daffodils," Sam says.

"They won't come up until spring," I say.

We hear a car pull up. I look at Sam. We both turn toward the street. "Dad," shouts Sam, crashing through the honeysuckle. Sam hugs Dad before he has a chance to get out of the car. He won't let go when Dad tries to walk. He puts his feet on Dad's shoes and Dad walks with him.

"Where's Sarah?" Dad asks. He has to. He has two kids.

Sam points, and the two of them head my way. I duck out quickly. The honeysuckle house would be crowded with so many people. Dad hugs me and I smell his office smell.

"Great haircut," he says.

My stomach flips. Tomorrow is a school day. I'll have to go to school looking like a boy.

"We have a surprise for you," Sam says, "but you can't see it until spring."

"How can I wait that long?" Dad puts his arm around Sam's skinny shoulders.

At dinner, Sam chatters away about a boy in his class, Dewayne, and how he has lived pretty close to us all this time but we never knew it. He's going to come over and play as soon as he asks his mom. Then Sam tries to get Dad to guess about the spring surprise.

"A bunny rabbit," says Dad.

Sam shakes his head. "I'll give you a hint. It's kind of round right now."

"A bowling ball," says Dad.

Sam laughs.

Dad puts his hand on Mom's. She pulls away. Dad thinks he can pop in and out and nothing will change while he's gone. He thinks if he asks us what's new, we can just fill him in. Simple. Like a business meeting. It starts and ends. I wish Dad's white car were a maroon Toyota. Victoria would be so happy to see me. I wouldn't ask her where she'd been. I wouldn't ask her to fill me in. We'd play all day and then, maybe, she'd say, "You know, Sarah, we moved in with my cousin."

"Oh, do you know where the pump is?" I ask Dad.

"I last saw it in the basement," he says. "Were you thinking of going on a bicycle ride?"

"Sort of," I answer.

"Want some company?" Dad asks.

"No thanks," I answer quickly. "I just wanted to ride around."

"I see," Dad says.

"Wow," Naomi says. "You sure got it chopped."

"Yup."

"Looks nice." She touches her own shoulder-length brown hair.

"I got tired of brushing it."

Naomi pulls her hair back into a ponytail, winds it around like a bun, then lets it fall. "I like playing with it," she says. What could I say? That I used to like playing with mine too, until Victoria left? That I don't want to look like Tina's sister?

Tina picks up her notebook and goes to the music room for English tutoring. "Doesn't seem like she's learning anything with that tutor," Naomi says. "She still can't say a word."

"Yes, she can. She just doesn't want to."

"Really? I never even heard her voice."

Miss Renfro is handing back our journals. I flip through the pages covered with words and arrows to the last few entries. Miss Renfro put a check next to the sentences about fall. Just a small ordinary check. I reread it. Buckeyes and crunchy leaves. I didn't write anything about pokeberry stew or Victoria leaving with one of the kittens and not the other.

I write my journal entry about getting my hair cut— the sound of the scissors, my black hair on the concrete steps, the small paws of the kitten as he batted my hair around. I don't even notice when Miss Renfro says it's time for recess.

Tina touches my elbow. I look up. Kids are lining up by the door. I shut my notebook. Tina waits for me to stand up and then follows me over to the line. As soon as we are outside, she goes over to the fence and points to a Mazda going slowly by the school. Inside are a man and a girl. "Your friend?" she asks.

I shake my head. "My friend is short."

"Short?"

"Small."

Tina nods. "My friend Mu Ying is big." With her hand she shows me that Mu Ying is tall.

"I thought you said you didn't know Chinese," Naomi says, joining us by the fence.

"I don't. We're talking in English."

Naomi stays to listen, but Tina won't talk when Naomi's there. She stares at the cars going by. Then she touches my shoulder and points to a car.

I shake my head.

"Do you guys talk in sign language?" Naomi asks.

"Sort of."

Naomi walks backward toward the football field. After a few steps she stops. I know she is listening for Tina's voice, but Tina waits until Naomi is gone.

"Victoria has black hair?" she asks, pulling on one of her pigtails.

"No. Blond."

Tina doesn't understand.

"Yellow." I change my mind. "White."

"White color," she says.

I nod.

"Mu Ying, black color." She forms scissors with her fingers. "Same you."

As soon as I get inside the front door, the phone rings. It's Naomi calling. She wants to know if I can walk over. "I have to baby-sit for my brother," I say quickly.

"Every day?" Naomi asks.

"Yup."

When I hang up, Mom's mouth is in a thin line. "Sarah, why did you say you had to baby-sit?" she asks.

"I don't want to go."

"I don't want you to use Sam as an excuse."

"Well, when you were working, I used to baby-sit." I try to save my lie.

"But I'm not working now precisely because I want you to have the freedom to do whatever you want after school without worrying about Sam." Mom's voice softens. "It wouldn't hurt you to have a friend." She touches my short hair. "Sarah, you can't just sit home and mope every afternoon."

"I'm not moping," I shout. "I wish you would go back to work." Once I start, I can't stop. "I liked it better when you were working. Me and Sam had fun by ourselves. Anyway, you can't make my friends for me."

My voice is so loud that Sam stops bouncing the ball. His face is scared. Mom's mouth is not in the thin straight line. It is soft and floppy as if she might cry. I don't want to see her mouth like that. I turn and run around to the back of the house to the honeysuckle house, to my seat inside the orphanage. Even without Victoria, I can play orphan. I can be an orphan all by myself.

The kitty comes in and settles on my lap. His fur gets wet from my tears and forms little clumps. He licks them with his tongue. Why does Mom think I'm moping when I'm petting the kitty or playing two-square with Sam? I wipe my face with the bottom of my T-shirt.

A car pulls up. I know without looking that it isn't a Toyota. It doesn't sound like it. I hear Dad's deep voice and Sam's high one. Sam is glad that Dad is not out of town this week, but that will just make it worse next week. Sam will wait for him even when he knows he's in Chicago. He'll watch by the window just in case Dad catches an earlier flight even if I tell him there are no earlier flights.

Through the honeysuckle branches I see Sam take Dad's hand before he is out of the car. They go into the house, and when they come back out, Sam is carrying a football. He bends down and holds the ball. Dad stands behind him. "Hike," says Dad. Sam shoots the ball like a bullet into Dad's hands.

It's cold in the honeysuckle house, but I don't want to go in. I mix the stew with a stick. The pokeberries are shriveled like raisins. Mom calls me for dinner. They won't let me stay out all night. Mom's voice is tight. "Sarah, come here this instant." Like Victoria's mom. She has run out of patience. Kitty opens his eyes and stares. When he yawns, I see all his sharp teeth. Soon he'll catch birds and mice. He stretches on his way off my lap, and I walk slowly into the house.

# T I N G

Ba Ba took the train back from Chicago. When he came into our apartment, he picked me up as if I were still a baby. "Ting, you've grown so tall." I looked hard at his face to see if I remembered it. When he set me down, he told Ma Ma that he didn't have the green card yet. He told her about a lawyer in Chicago who took his money but did nothing. He waited in lots of long lines in many offices, but still no green card.

Ma Ma sighed. Then she told Ba Ba how well I had been doing for the first two weeks in my new school. Ba Ba hardly seemed to hear. Ma Ma told him she had another house to clean and she was earning lots of money. She showed him an envelope full of dollars. That made Ba Ba happy. She also told him about the English class; she had already signed up.

Ba Ba looked at her sternly. "How much does it cost to take a class?"

Ma Ma didn't answer.

He asked her again.

"I don't know the exact price," she said. Then Ba Ba picked up the envelope full of dollars and put it into his pocket.

We had spicy noodles for dinner. Ma Ma got them at the Chinese food store. They looked like Po Po's, but the smell was different, so I wrinkled my nose. "Food is to eat, not to smell," Ma Ma said.

After dinner Ba Ba turned on the television. He said that if we watched a lot of television, we would learn English, but he kept changing the channels. I tried to talk to Ma Ma instead of watching, but then he turned the volume up higher. Ma Ma said it was too loud, we might bother the neighbors. Ba Ba turned off the television and smoked three cigarettes in a row. Then he pushed the table against the wall and started practicing kung fu like he did with Uncle in the park in front of our building. He kicked and shouted and kicked again. The neighbors would wonder what was going on in our apartment.

When I went to bed, the smoke was in my covers. I wished Ba Ba had stayed in Chicago. Then I wouldn't hear him kicking and shouting so loud. When he and Uncle practiced kung fu in Shanghai, I used to sit on the park bench and watch them move together. Their shouts were small in the park outside. But in our small apartment Ba Ba's voice was big.

A week later, Ba Ba got a call from his friend. He told Ba Ba to go back to Chicago right away. He had a new green-card lawyer. While we were waiting for the train, Ba Ba smoked a lot. The smoke got into my throat and made me cough.

When Ba Ba hugged me to say goodbye, I couldn't wait for him to leave so the smoke would get out of my face.

Ma Ma was quiet on the bus ride back to our apartment. She shut her eyes, but she wasn't sleeping. I looked out the window at all the houses going by. It started to drizzle, and the raindrops looked like they were going up the glass. If Uncle were there, I could ask him why they looked that way.

"Ma Ma."

"Hmm?"

"When can Uncle come?"

"I don't know."

"But when?"

"After Ba Ba gets the green card and we can save money for the airplane ticket, then he can come."

"Can Po Po come too?"

"And who will take care of Hong?"

I forgot about my cousin. "Okay. Uncle can come by himself. He can sleep in my room."

"Maybe by then we will have a small house," Ma Ma said.

The houses were going by so fast. One after the other, so many small houses.

After that, whenever I walked home from school, I looked at all the houses along the way. I liked the one with the weathervane on top. That would be a good one to have so we would know which way the wind was blowing. When we got home, I drew a picture of the house to send to Uncle.

•

Ma Ma had English class in the afternoon, so she wasn't home when I came back from school. She gave me a key to the apartment and told me to do my homework first and then watch television. We had to write one sentence for each spelling word. The words were easy, like *lonely* and *several*. But what should I write? Outside the window I could see the dumpster. A cat was walking around it. I wrote *The cat is lonely*. Then I wrote *There are several stars in the sky*. My English teacher in Shanghai had taught me harder words. I turned on the television. There was a blond lady talking and laughing. Her voice was too sharp.

I turned off the television and went out to the jungle. I had learned to climb higher in the mulberry tree. From the top I could look into the dumpster and see what people threw away, like pieces of chicken and flowerpots. When my legs got tired, I crouched in the shade and pulled up some of the grass with my fingers so I would have room for more plants.

"Ting, what are you doing?" Ma Ma jerked me up by my arm. "I told you to stay inside until I got home." Ma Ma tried to brush the mud off my pants. "The landlord will get mad if you pull up the grass. Do you want the landlord to make us move?"

"Move where?"

Ma Ma pulled me along into the apartment.

In November the wind turned cold and I had to wear a coat to school. Luckily Po Po had sent me a warm one with a hood and a small rabbit on the sleeve. I was so proud to wear it to school, but when I got to the edge of the playground, a girl said, "How's your little bunny, Tina?" She turned to her friend and laughed.

The bunny on my sleeve looked at me with its big round eyes.

"Its eyes are bigger than hers," the friend said. They laughed so loud. The first girl put her fingers in the corners of her eyes and pulled. Her friend copied.

Sarah was over by the fence. I tried to slip past, but the first girl grabbed at the bunny. I could hardly feel it through the padding of the jacket. Still, tears came to my eyes. I would not cry at school. I would spit on the girl, right in her face. *Show the world that Chinese children are good.* The saliva pooled in my mouth. I clenched my teeth and ran past the girls to the fence.

Even in the morning before school, Sarah was reading. She was always reading. She never even looked up when I came. She would rather read her book than talk to me. I watched the cars go by. So many cars in America, black ones and brown ones and white trucks. "There is a red car," I said.

Sarah looked up for a minute. "It's not hers." She marked her place on the page with her finger.

All morning I barely looked up from my worksheets. If I looked down everyone would stop staring at me. The math problems were easy. Uncle had taught me all that even before I learned it at school. He showed me and Hong how to multiply big numbers when we were five. Hong hated it, but I always asked for more math problems to practice. I looked over at Sarah's paper. Her numbers were messy, but the answers were the same as mine. I put my face close to the paper so I could see better and I did all the problems before the bell rang.

Sarah finished her book during language arts, so she had nothing to read at recess.

"Tina, can you teach me something in Chinese?" she asked.

Why should I teach her? Just because she forgot to bring another book to read?

"Can you teach me how to write 'friend'?" she asked.

I could make a bunch of little lines and tell her it meant friend. She would never know one squiggle from the next. But what if she found out? What if she already knew a little Chinese? Sarah asked me again, slowly. "Can you please teach me how to write 'friend'?" Her face was smooth and clear. Slowly I wrote the two characters for *peng you* on the back of my notebook. She tried to copy it, but she made the lines too long. I showed her again. She practiced until she could remember the strokes in the right order.

"Is this right?" Sarah asked.

"Very good," I said.

"I'll practice at home," she said. Then she gave me the book she'd finished. "It's a really good story about a boy who survives in the forest."

"The boy is alone?"

"He knows which berries to eat and how to hunt and everything."

"How does he know that?"

"Partly from his dad. Partly from library books."

I thumbed through the pages. "It is very difficult."

"I can help you," she said. "I'm reading the sequel."

"Sequel?"

"The next book."

I started the first page. I read slowly but I could understand. Sarah's eyes moved like lightning across the pages. Maybe someday I could read fast like that.

"The boy in the story is very smart," I told Sarah when the bell rang.

"You can take the book home if you want to."

All afternoon when Sarah finished her work, she practiced writing *peng you*. At the end of the day she could write the characters almost perfectly.

Ma Ma told me not to go out to the jungle anymore because it was too cold. I would get a sore throat from the damp air. I might even catch pneumonia. She would hurry home from class as fast as she could.

I still went out to check on my plants. They might die if I didn't water them. I took water from the kitchen in a cup and poured it on the stems. The cup was small, so I had to make lots of trips and some water spilled on the rug.

A lady came out and threw something into the dumpster. She didn't say "Hi" or "What are you doing here?" or anything. In China, Mr. Zhen's mother would say, "Ting, it's too cold, go inside." Mrs. Tang would say, "Ting, your jacket is dirty. Ma Ma will be angry. Let me help you wash it." Here nobody said anything to anyone.

I tried to wipe the mud off my sleeve, but it didn't come out. I hurried inside so Ma Ma wouldn't find me, and I hung my jacket on the hook with the sleeve inside to hide the mud. I passed the mirror in the front hall and stopped to take the extra rubber bands out of my hair. How would it look if I wore it loose like the girls at school? Or in one ponytail?

"Ting, don't play with your hair," Ma Ma said sharply. I hadn't even heard her come in. She picked the rubber bands off the floor. Then she parted my hair with her fingers and fixed the pigtails. "You cannot leave your hair loose. Loose hair gets lice."

Ma Ma took off her shoes and sat on the sofa with her feet up. Her ankles were swollen. She rubbed them with her hands. Then she saw the spot on the rug.

"Ting, what is that on the rug?"

"I don't know."

Ma Ma rubbed her face with her hands. "The landlord will be angry if we ruin his apartment."

"I didn't ruin anything."

"Now you sound like an American girl, talking back to her mother. Go and clean the spot on the rug."

I got a sponge and rubbed at the spot so hard that bits of sponge peeled off. My eyes were watery, but I wouldn't let Ma Ma see. Why did she bring me to America if the children in America got lice and talked back to their mothers?

When I got home from school on Friday, Ma Ma was there with a Chinese lady I'd never met. Ma Ma introduced her to me as Auntie Daisy. I knew she was not my real aunt. In China I called all my parents' friends auntie this and uncle that.

"Oh, Ting, your mother told me all about you," Auntie Daisy said in perfect English. Her voice was big. Her smile was without the white teeth of American ladies. She touched my cheek like Po Po's friends in Shanghai. "You are very tall," she said, "not short like me. And Ma Ma says you learn English so fast."

Ma Ma nodded proudly. She gave me rice porridge with sour pickles for a snack. While I ate, she and Auntie Daisy talked in Chinese, getting louder and louder. Their voices rose and fell like Po Po and her friend Auntie Yuan in Shanghai. Auntie Daisy said how funny it was that she and Ma Ma lived only a block apart but had never seen each other before. She turned to me and said, "I was cleaning my front window this morning, and I saw a lady hurrying to catch the bus, and I said to myself, 'Now that lady must be Chinese,' so I dropped my rag and went right over to the bus stop."

"And I almost missed my English class," Ma Ma said.

"Just think, we lived only a few blocks away from each other in Shanghai too," Auntie said.

"Small world," said Ma Ma.

Auntie Daisy sighed. "But sometimes it seems so big." She looked out the window. "You are lucky, you have Ting here with you. But my boys grew up and moved so far away. Better to have a daughter. A daughter stays home, close to her mother."

"But a daughter is harder to raise than a son."

Auntie Daisy shook her head. "A daughter is easier, not wild."

"Ting is wild like a boy. She gets so dirty, you wouldn't believe she is a girl."

Auntie Daisy smiled. "That's good. A girl in this world needs to be strong."

"Maybe you are right," Ma Ma said.

Auntie Daisy stood up and smoothed her skirt. She looked older than Ma Ma because of the lines in her face, but she was thinner and she had a skirt like a young lady. "Better eat your rice," she said to me in English, coming over to the table. "So you can grow even taller." She laughed. "Not small like Auntie."

I put the chopsticks to my mouth. I wished Auntie would stay and talk to Ma Ma so I could listen to their voices rise and fall and to Ma Ma laughing. Chinese, English, Auntie moved back and forth, mixing, not caring. She told Ma Ma about her husband, who died a few years ago. He worked for a big company. They had two sons. She always wished she had at least one daughter, but her husband said two sons were plenty of children.

"Maybe you will have a granddaughter someday," Ma Ma said. "And now you have Ting like an extra daughter for you."

Ma Ma was in a good mood after Auntie left. "Such good luck to meet a friend," she said. I told her about Sarah who had a Chinese face but didn't know Chinese words and who had a little brother, Sam, but I didn't tell her about the girls who pulled their eyes and grabbed the bunny on my jacket. Ma Ma would go out and buy me a new jacket without a bunny. Then she would have to clean more houses to save more dollars in the envelope.

**S
A
R
A
H**

**Right before Thanksgiving break, I** go over to Naomi's house after school. Her mother isn't there, and her sister is on the phone in the back room with the door shut. Naomi takes me up to her room. We look at a teen magazine with pictures of girls in woolly sweaters and ski pants. We cut them out and make them into paper dolls.

"I wish I could be a model someday, but my sister says you have to have really long legs," Naomi says. I look at Naomi's long nose and small eyes. Even if her legs were longer, she wouldn't look like the girls in the magazines at all. "Hey, you have long legs. Maybe you could be a model," she says, looking at my legs, which reach halfway across the floor of the room.

"I'm Chinese," I say quickly.

"Well, so is she." Naomi points to a girl in the magazine.

"I don't want to be a model. I couldn't stand taking all those clothes on and off."

"I wish I were Chinese," Naomi says suddenly, moving her head over so we can see her reflection next to mine in the mirror. "I mean, my face is just so ordinary."

I can't believe Naomi said that. She wishes she were Chinese, but she doesn't know what she's talking about. Would she want the art teacher to call her Emma for a whole year? Would she want people to think Tina was her twin sister? My short hair is sticking out, since I hardly ever brush it anymore. I smooth it with my hand. "My face is ordinary too, in China," I say.

"But I mean here you're not ordinary." Naomi says.

When we finish our dolls, I tell Naomi I'd better head home. "I'm glad you could come over," she says. We wave to each other until the bend in the street. The sun is low and my shadow is long. Funny how the days are short like winter but the air feels as if fall wants to stay forever. The afternoon went by fast. It was kind of fun making the paper dolls.

Sam comes running down the hill to meet me. "Guess what?" His face is sweaty and flushed. "I was out tossing the football with Dewayne and we saw this maroon car pull up."

"Was it her?"

Sam nods. "Her mom ran into their house to get a few things."

"Did she take the kitten?"

"Nope. He's sleeping on our back porch. She just went in to get some jackets and stuff."

"Did Victoria get out of the car?"

"Yup. She was waiting for you in the honeysuckle

house, but then her mom said they had to hurry."

I feel a lump in my throat. If I hadn't gone to Naomi's, I would have been there. I wouldn't have missed Victoria. I would have been playing orphan or boxcar instead of cutting dumb dolls out of magazines.

"Did you talk to her?" I ask. My voice is crackly.

"I told her you'd be back soon," Sam says. "Oh, and she said we could name the kitten whatever we wanted."

"Did she say anything else?"

Sam thinks for a minute. "She said they moved to Daniel's."

"Who's Daniel?"

Sam shrugs. "I don't know."

"You could have asked."

Once Victoria told me that her mother had a boyfriend named Dan. That could be the Daniel. But then it could be somebody else. I head back to the honeysuckle house. Something looks different. The twine is still there. I look at my stone seat, and right in the middle of it is the biggest, shiniest buckeye I have ever seen. I hold it in my hands, still fresh and warm from the sun. I know that Victoria left it there for me.

I put the buckeye into my pocket. Tomorrow I'll show it to Tina.


"I have a letter from Mu Ying," Tina tells me as soon as she sees me in the morning. She unfolds a piece of very thin paper covered with Chinese writing and shows me the characters for her Chinese name, Ting.

"Is that your real name?" I ask her.

"My Chinese name. My American name is Tina."

I take the big buckeye out of my pocket. "From my friend," I say.

"Victoria?" she asks.

I nod.

Tina hands back the buckeye. "Victoria came home?"

I shake my head. "My brother said she and her mother stopped in to get their jackets. I wasn't home."

"She will come again soon," says Tina. Then she points to the buckeye. "What is it?"

"A buckeye," I say.

"Buckeye," she says. "We can eat the buckeye?"

I hold my stomach. "We cannot eat buckeyes."

Tina sits on the ground and takes out her notebook. She shows me a letter she's writing to Mu Ying. "Sarah," she says, pointing to my name. Then I see where she wrote the two characters for *peng you*.

I want to learn more Chinese characters, but Tina is busy writing her letter. She makes all the tiny lines quickly across the paper. She's lucky. She can write to her friend. I don't even know where my friend is.

After school Tina is standing in front of the school building with tears running down her cheeks. Miss Miller, our student teacher, is trying to find out what's wrong, but Tina won't talk. The school buses have already left. Sam and Dewayne are walking up ahead.

"Where's your mom?" I ask.

Tina keeps crying without making any noise at all. Miss Miller steps back.

"Where is your mother?" I ask again.

Tina swallows. "I don't know."

"Was she supposed to meet you here?"

Tina nods.

I look at Miss Miller. "If it's okay she can come home with me."

Miss Miller tells me to wait while she calls Tina's mother and my mother. Tina's sweater is twisted. One of her rubber bands is loose. I wind it around once more and straighten out her sweater just like her mother does each day. When Miss Miller comes back, she says, "Sarah, your mom said it was okay for Tina to come over. I left a message for Tina's mother to call you when she gets home. Can you tell her that in Chinese?"

"I don't speak it," I say, wishing for the first time that I really could.

"I thought you were talking to her on the playground," Miss Miller says.

"I was. But we were talking in English." I turn to Tina. "Let's go to my house." I point to my watch. "Your mother will come later."

Tina takes a deep breath and wipes her cheek with the back of her hand. I take her Lucky Dog book bag and put it on one shoulder and my own book bag on the other. "Come on," I say, taking her hand.

I pull Tina along. The wind is blowing the leaves around. They form a whirlwind by the curb. I try to catch one and miss. Tina catches a yellow elm leaf on her first try.

"That's good luck," I say.

Tina looks confused.

I point to the word "luck" on the Lucky Dog book bag. "You will have good luck. You will be happy," I say.

Tina smiles. "Yes," she says. The whole way up the hill, we keep trying to catch leaves. Tina takes a curly oak leaf out of my hair. "Good luck," she says, even though the leaf caught me. Then she picks something up off the sidewalk. "A buckeye," she says. There are buckeyes all over the sidewalk and the street. Some are still nestled in their shells. I show Tina how sometimes there are two or three or even four buckeyes in one shell. "So many baby buckeyes," she says. We stuff them into our pockets until we can hardly walk. Tina takes off her sweater. We tie knots in the sleeves and fill them with more and more buckeyes.

When Tina sees Mom, she starts talking to her in Chinese. "My mom doesn't speak Chinese," I say, stopping her in the middle of a sentence.

Tina lifts her eyebrows. "America?" she asks.

I nod.

"Your mother called," my mom says to Tina. "She'll be here at five thirty."

Mom offers us cookies and milk, but Tina wants only a glass of water. We sit out on the front steps. Sam and Dewayne are tossing the football. Kitty lunges at a leaf, catches it, and brings it to me like a prize.

"Good luck," says Tina. Then she looks over at the house next door.

"That's Victoria's house," I say.

"She will come home soon," she says. "Good luck." Then I understand. All the leaves we caught mean that

Victoria will be home soon. We head around back to the honeysuckle house. Kitty comes in and rolls in the dry leaves by my feet. Tina looks scared.

"He's a baby cat," I say, petting him on his belly. "A kitten." He reaches for my hand, grabs it with his paws, and then bounds away. We dump all of our buckeyes into a big pile in the middle of the honeysuckle house and bury our hands in their coolness. Then we count them together, Tina in Chinese and me in English. "Fifty-six," I say.

"*Wu shi liu*," Tina says. She teaches me to count all the way to one hundred in Chinese.

Tina shows me a game we can play with the buckeyes. You throw one buckeye up and pick up more before you catch it, kind of like jacks. Tina's hands are quick and sure. "I play with Mu Ying," she says.

"Do you have buckeyes in China?" I ask.

"We have rocks," Tina says.

"Hey, what are you guys doing?" Sam pokes his head inside the house.

"Fifty-six buckeyes." I show him the pile.

"I bet me and Dewayne can find more," he says, grabbing Dewayne by his T-shirt and heading around the house.

The wind is picking up. Big gray clouds are moving fast. "It might rain," I say to Tina.

She stands up and dusts off the back of her skirt. Then she points at her watch. "Ma Ma is coming," she says, shaking out her sweater and putting it on. I zip up her book bag and help her put it onto her shoulders. We go out of the honeysuckle house to wait.

At five twenty-five, Tina sees her mother turn the corner. "Ma Ma," she shouts, running down the street. Together they come toward me.

"So sorry, so sorry," her mother says. Mom comes out. Tina's mother says thank you over and over. Then she says she had to work late, she tried to hurry."

"No problem," Mom says. "We are so happy Sarah has a new friend."

Tina reaches into her jacket pocket and pulls out a buckeye. "Buckeye," she says to her mother. Then she explains something about the buckeye in Chinese.

After they're gone, Mom pulls a leaf out of my hair. "Did you have a nice time with Tina?" she asks.

I wish Mom didn't ask me things like that. I don't know what to say. Tina isn't really my friend yet. I hardly know her. Her English isn't good enough to pretend anything. Maybe she isn't even the pretending type. She's afraid of the kitty. But I like sitting with her in the honeysuckle house and playing jacks with the buckeyes.

"It was fine," I say, heading inside to do my homework. As soon as I open my notebook, I see the *peng you* paper. Suddenly I have an idea. I copy the characters in black marker on light blue paper. Then I write *friend* in my best cursive underneath. I put the paper in a plastic bag to protect it and take it out to the honeysuckle house. Kitty is asleep on the dish towel on the stone. I set the paper in the middle of the buckeye pile so that just the top sticks out. If Victoria comes again when I'm not home, she'll be sure to find it.

**T**
**I**
**N**
**G**

**At the beginning of December, Ba Ba finally got a letter** from Immigration. He read it over many times and put it into his pocket.

"What does the letter say?" I asked.

"They are processing my green-card application."

I couldn't believe we had been waiting so long just for that. Ba Ba said the real green card was sure to come soon. He would stay in Cincinnati with us for a while.

Ba Ba bought the newspaper and started looking through the job ads, circling the ones that he thought might be good. While he looked, he smoked cigarettes. Ma Ma cooked special fish with green onions to celebrate the letter. Then she showed Ba Ba my report card with all A's. The teacher had written on the bottom, *Tina is progressing very quickly in English. Her math skills are excellent.* Ba Ba patted my head. "Very smart girl," he said. Ma Ma copied my grades in a letter to send to Po Po and Uncle in Shanghai.

"Why don't you write a letter to Hong?" Ma Ma said. "I bet she misses you."

I knew Hong didn't miss me at all. She always said Uncle liked me better than his own daughter. If I wrote a letter to Uncle, Hong might be mad. Instead I wrote a letter to Mu Ying.

When my letter was finished, I wanted to go outside and look around in the dumpster.

"Can I go outside?" I asked.

"It's too muddy outside, Ting," Ma Ma said.

I went to get my jacket.

"Ting." Ma Ma's voice was sharp. I dropped my jacket on the floor. "Go to your room."

I lay down on my bed and pulled the sheet over my head. When I woke up, it was dark. Outside the small window the moon was only a sliver. It looked like a smile, like the girl's smile when she saw the bunny on my sleeve, like Miss Renfro when she said I was doing well. Only Sarah didn't smile because she was always looking for Victoria.

Saturday morning I stayed home while Ma Ma left to clean houses and Ba Ba went out to look for a job. Maybe Ba Ba could be a cashier. He was good with numbers. He used to be an accountant in a big firm in China. He could add faster in his head than other people could with a calculator. Ma Ma told me to clean the kitchen while she was gone and then watch television.

I wiped the sink. I wouldn't touch the oven. It could be hot and dangerous. Then I went outside to check on my plants. The sun was warm on my back so I took off my jacket. The plants were growing just fine. I would tell

Po Po that I had a small garden in America.

The dumpster was almost empty. The only thing I found was some nails. Those might be useful someday if I built something out of wood. I put them into my pocket and climbed into the mulberry tree to wait for Ba Ba. When I saw him turn the corner, I ran in through the back door.

"Did you find a job?" I asked.

Ba Ba shook his head. He lit a cigarette and inhaled deeply. "The problem is my English. As soon as I ask to see the manager, they say, 'Excuse me?' So I repeat the same thing ten times and they still shake their heads." Ba Ba turned to me. "Ting, how do you say it?"

Ba Ba practiced each word. *May–I–please–speak–to–the–manager?* He got the words more or less right. The problem was putting them together. His voice went up and down when it shouldn't. It sounded like nonsense Chinese. After he tried for half an hour, his throat was sore.

"I can go with you," I said. "I can tell the manager how fast you add numbers in your head."

Ba Ba sighed and smoked two more cigarettes.

We set out the next Saturday morning. Ba Ba wore black pants and a white shirt. I wore a red dress that was almost too small. Ma Ma fixed my pigtails with four rubber bands in each, in different colors.

"Two rubber bands are enough," I said.

"No," Ma Ma said. "You don't want to look like a mess. Hurry. Ba Ba is waiting. Go get your jacket."

My jacket was not in the closet or in my room. I tried

to remember the last time I had worn it. Suddenly I knew. While Ma Ma was in the bathroom, I ran out back. There was my jacket on the ground by the dumpster. How could I have left the bunny out for so many nights? I shook the jacket as hard as I could and put my arms into the damp sleeves. When Ma Ma wasn't home I would wash it in the sink. I would wash the bunny's chubby face.

We tried the meat market first. They weren't hiring. Next we went to the grocery store.

"May we speak to the manager, please?" I asked.

"You're looking at him," answered a big man with a red face. "So, who wants the job, you or your daddy?"

"My father can add very fast."

"And you talk very fast," the man said. I couldn't tell from his face if his smile was friendly or mad. "So, are you from China? Japan?"

"Shanghai, China."

"Maybe you can teach me a little Chinese. That is what you speak over there, isn't it? I mean, all I know so far is chop suey."

"Yes, yes," said Ba Ba.

"You have permission to work in this country?" the man asked.

Ba Ba looked confused.

"He's asking about the green card," I said quickly in Chinese.

"Yes, yes." Ba Ba took the letter out of his pocket.

The man read it over quickly. "What kind of work did you do back home?"

"My father was an accountant for a big company," I said.

"I see," said the man. He scratched the top of his bald head and considered. "I'll tell you what," he said, handing Ba Ba an application. "Fill this out, and we'll give it a try. But remember, it's a trial. Temporary. We'll give it a couple of weeks and go from there. How about that?"

I translated for Ba Ba. "Thank you, thank you," he said, holding on to the man's hand and bowing at the same time. I wanted to tell Ba Ba that in America people didn't bow and that he should let go of the man's hand, but the man just smiled patiently.

"Tomorrow at eight," the man said.

"Yes, yes," Ba Ba said, still bowing as the man turned to leave.

Ba Ba was quiet on the way home. I couldn't tell if he was happy about the job or not. He told me that when he got the green card, he would find a good job in a big company like he had in China.

"Why did you quit your job in China?" I asked.

"There is opportunity in America," he said.

"What opportunity?"

"A better future. A better future for you," he said.

"What is a better future?"

"Ting, don't talk so much. When you talk you forget to walk." Ba Ba pulled me along.

When we went inside, I wanted to draw airplanes, but Ba Ba wanted me to do thirty math problems that he had written out for me. I did two of them but then went back to working on the tail of my 747. It was too high. The airplane I flew on did not have a tail so high. I erased it and started over. Uncle would fly to America on a 747 with a tail that was straight. Ba Ba's cigarettes were making me cough again.

"You did only two problems?" Ba Ba's voice was hard. He took my airplane picture, wadded it up into a ball, and tossed it into the garbage can. "Now you will finish the problems," he said.

"But I want to—"

Ba Ba raised his hand and I thought he might hit me. "Just because you know English, do you think you know more than your father?" He shook his head.

The water in my eyes made the numbers blurry. How could I solve a problem if it was all blurry on the paper? I rubbed my eyes and put my face close to the paper. Then I wrote the numbers in neat columns. When Ma Ma came home, I was still working. Ba Ba was practicing kung fu kicks in the living room.

"Did he get a job?" she whispered to me.

"Yes," I said, not looking up.

I wished that Ma Ma had never sent for me so I would still be in Shanghai with Uncle and Po Po. Mu Ying would look for me on the playground, and Uncle would never crumple my pictures.

When Ba Ba went to work on Sunday, I went with Ma Ma to the house she was cleaning. The bus ride took forever. Ma Ma closed her eyes, but I wasn't tired.

"Ma Ma, did you clean houses in Shanghai?" I asked.

"I cleaned our apartment."

"I mean, did you clean other people's houses?"

"In Shanghai everybody cleaned their own small apartment."

"Then how did you earn money?"

"I was a secretary in the office. Do you remember?"

I shook my head.

Ma Ma put her head back on the seat.

"Was it fun to be a secretary?"

"No, Ting, it was a boring job."

"Worse than cleaning houses?"

Ma Ma didn't answer right away. "Not better, not worse," she said finally.

"Why did you have that boring job?"

"I wanted to go to the university, but my score was too low." Ma Ma took my hand in hers. "But in America everybody can study."

"Study what?"

Ma Ma looked out the window. "First I will learn English. Then maybe I will be a nurse."

When I was six I broke my arm. The nurse at the hospital wrapped it in white gauze. When she moved my arm, it hurt so much. I tried to imagine Ma Ma like that nurse in a white uniform with a small white hat.

A lady got on the bus with three little children. The two girls sat on her lap and the boy sat beside her on the seat. "In America people have many children," I said.

"In China we can have only one," Ma Ma said.

"Why?"

"China is too crowded already. Remember all the people in the street?"

"What if you have two?"

Ma Ma didn't answer right away. "Two is not allowed. Two is too many."

"But what if you have two?"

"I already told you, Ting."

Ma Ma closed her eyes. The little girls on the seat in front of us were hitting each other. If there were only one, they wouldn't be fighting. There wouldn't even be the little sisters. The bus stopped abruptly. "Oh, Ting, we forgot to get off." Ma Ma stood up and pulled me down the back steps of the bus.

We walked up a wide street with big trees on both sides that met in the middle. The houses were so far apart that you could hardly see your neighbor. I would be scared to live in such a big house. If you yelled, there would be nobody to hear you. Ten families could live in such a big house. Maybe twenty. When we got to a tall yellow house, we walked down the brick sidewalk and around to the back door. Ma Ma had a key to get in.

She started on the kitchen counter and told me to clean the sinks, but when I was done, she did them over again. Why would one family need two sinks? In Shanghai we washed our dishes in the bathroom. Uncle heated water on the hot plate and put it in a big thermos to keep it warm.

I wandered into the living room. There were shelves covered with crystal vases and sculptures and polished rocks. I picked up a wooden animal that looked like a buffalo.

I had never seen a real buffalo, but I had seen them in pictures. The wood was smooth and light. I touched it to my cheek. It would be fun to carve animals like that. On the bottom were somebody's initials. Carving wood would be a better job than being a cashier at a grocery store or cleaning big houses. If I had a knife like Uncle's, I could carve wood or stone. I could carve name stamps like Uncle or I could carve animals. Instead of a plane ticket or a house I would save my money for a carving knife.

"Ting, don't touch." Ma Ma's voice was so loud I almost dropped the buffalo. "If you break something in this house, then what? Who pays for it?" I put the animal gently on the shelf. Ma Ma went back to the kitchen.

There was a giraffe on the top shelf, but from where I was, I could hardly see it. I rolled a chair out of the studio, pushed it up to the shelf, and stood up. The giraffe was carved out of light wood, but it had dark spots painted all over. Or were they carved too? I leaned over to pick up the giraffe and look at its spots. The chair rolled as I leaned. I grabbed the shelf to catch my balance. It tipped and everything on it went crashing to the floor.

I didn't move. Ma Ma was in the kitchen. The house was so big. Would she hear? I waited. No footsteps. I got off the chair and looked at the mess on the floor. The wooden animals were fine except for a small nick on the buffalo's front leg. One of the vases had landed on the rug and didn't break. But the crystal one was in a million pieces all over the floor. I found some tissues and started picking up the glass, careful not to cut myself. I took lots of tissues and wrapped up the glass so nobody would see it and put it into the garbage can. Then I put everything back up on the shelf and spread it out so you couldn't tell where the vase had been.

"Ting?" There was Ma Ma in her maid's dress with a mop in her hands. "Just checking on you," she said. My throat felt swollen shut. If I talked, I would cry. I could tell Ma Ma what happened. But she said not to touch anything. The vase would be very expensive. How could we ever pay for it? Ma Ma would have to clean more and more houses. "Why don't you sit at the table and write a letter to Uncle and Po Po and Hong," Ma Ma suggested.

I didn't write anything. I didn't draw either. I sat at the desk and felt the smooth wood with my palms. Someday I would make furniture. Tables and chairs and desks like this one with smooth wood. I didn't look at the shelf or the garbage can or anything but my hands. There was a piece of string on the desk. I tied it into a loop and did Jacob's Ladder over and over. I could do it so fast, faster even than Mu Ying.

"Tina? Is that your name?"

I turned around. The lady who owned the house was setting a big cardboard box on the floor.

"Here are some clothes my daughter never wears. I'm sure some of them will fit you." She pulled a fuzzy white sweater out of the box and held it out. "Here. Try this on."

Slowly I took off the gray sweater Po Po had knitted for me. The lady helped me pull the white sweater over my head. "Perfect," she said, tossing my old sweater onto the floor. "Try on the rest. What doesn't fit we'll give to charity."

When the lady left, I opened the box. T-shirts with English words, sweatshirts with hoods, velvet pants. I picked my gray sweater off the floor and folded it neatly. Po Po had knitted it in the evening while she and Uncle watched the late-night comedy on television. They laughed so loud. In the morning, my sweater was done.

I picked up a blue sweatshirt that said *University of Arizona* across the front. It still had the tags from the store. Why was the lady's daughter giving it away? Was there something wrong with it? Would kids laugh at the University of Arizona? I would not wear these new clothes.

As soon as we got home, the telephone rang. My stomach tightened. It was probably the lady calling to fire Ma Ma because of the crystal vase. Then Ma Ma would have to find other houses to clean to pay for the vase. Ba Ba would be so angry. He would tell Ma Ma to quit her class. Ma Ma was talking in English. "Yes, yes, thank you. Thank you very much." Thank you for what? When Ma Ma hung up, she said the lady had found some more clothes for me. "She said we should remind her next time, okay, Ting?"

I swallowed hard. "Yes. I will remember."

The day before winter break, Miss Renfro asked us to write about a holiday tradition in our homes. In Shanghai, we celebrated the New Year with sticks you can light with fire, but I didn't know the word in English. We also got money in red envelopes. Uncle always gave me the most beautiful red envelope with lots of coins inside. I started to write about the fire sticks, but what if Miss Renfro read my paper to the class? She did that sometimes. Everyone would look at me. Chinese girls play with fire, they would say. I erased my sentence. I would write something about Christmas. That was what all the kids were talking about—Christmas wish lists and Christmas vacations. I wrote, "Christmas is my favorite holiday. For Christmas this year I am getting a pocketknife. We are going on vacation to the beach." After the words were on the page, I wondered why I wrote them. We didn't even celebrate Christmas.

Sarah wrote fast. When she was done, she showed me her paper. She wrote that every New Year's Day, she and her mother and father and Sam went on a New Year's hike in the woods. Sometimes it was cold and the creek was frozen. Sometimes it was raining. After the hike they made a big fire and cooked lunch. When they got home, they took all the ornaments off their Christmas tree and planted it in the back yard.

Sarah wasn't afraid to write the truth. She didn't worry about Miss Renfro reading her paragraph out loud or the cross-outs and arrows. In China, I didn't worry either. My compositions were the best in the class. My teacher said maybe I would be a writer someday.

"Tina." Miss Renfro called me into the hall. Could she know about the vase? My legs shook so that I could hardly walk. She put her arm around my shoulders and said my

English was getting better so fast that after the winter break I didn't need to go to special English class anymore. "Your parents must be so proud of you," she said, smiling close to my face.

"Thank you," I mumbled, not letting my eyes meet hers. I wanted to tell her that really my English was still bad. Many times I could not find the right words. They were stuck in my stomach, all those lying words.

Sarah was reading by the fence. I didn't want to interrupt her, but where else could I go? Three boys who sat in the back of the class were watching me. "Ching, Chang, Chung," one said. I kept on walking. They shouted together, "Ching, Chang, Chung." Everyone heard their loud voices. Sarah too. Together we could hit those boys. They were small and skinny. My Ba Ba knew kung fu. He could kick those boys so hard. I kept walking until I got to the fence. Sarah didn't look up, but her eyes were not moving across the words. Our arms touched. I put my hand in my pocket and there was my string. I put the first step of the string game on my fingers.

Sarah's eyes met mine, and I could see that they were watery. She put her fingers through the X's and around. We went back and forth for a long time.

"Do you play this in China?" Sarah whispered.

"Yes. I play with Mu Ying."

"I used to play with Victoria," Sarah said. "She's really fast."

"Mu Ying is fast too."

I hooked the string with my baby finger, but it fell off and made a knot.

"Let's make up our own string game," Sarah said. Soon we were all tangled up in the string. Sarah's sticking-out hair tickled my face. Our hands were knotted together.

"We could use this string to tie up those boys," she said.

"Tie up?"

"You know," she said. "We can capture Ching, Chang, and Chung."

I smiled. "Yes, Ching, Chang, and Chung."

"And take them to a deserted island."

"And we can leave them."

"Without food or water."

"And they do not know berries to eat and not eat."

"And they eat some poison ones."

"Yes."


When I got home, Ma Ma was still in class and Ba Ba was at work. There was a small package by our front door. I picked it up and set it on the kitchen table. The return address said only *Shanghai, China.* Maybe I should wait for Ma Ma or Ba Ba before I opened it. I traced the letters with my finger. *Tina Liang.* The package was definitely addressed to me.

I took a knife out of the drawer and slit the tape. Under two layers of crumpled newspaper was a small wooden box. I unlatched the tiny hinges and lifted the lid. There was a short note from Uncle that said, *A small present to remind you of home.* Under the note were four ivory-handled carving tools. Each tool had its own velvet hollow in the box. One by one I took them out: two Ushaped chisels, a file, and a knife. They were so perfect. How did Uncle know exactly what I wanted? Someday I would learn to carve birds and frogs and name stamps. Uncle would show me. I closed the lid of the box, and for a second I thought I heard Uncle's footsteps in the hallway, but the steps went past our apartment to the next door down.

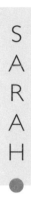

S
A
R
A
H

**Our winter break is cold and rainy. If only all that rain** were snow, me and Sam could fly down the hill behind the school on our sleds. But it's not, so I read six books and try to teach Sam to whistle. He puckers his mouth every which way, but he can't make a sound.

When we get back to school, most of the girls have on sweaters and turtlenecks that they got for Christmas. It's raining, so we wait for Miss Renfro outside the door of her room. I look around for Tina. When she sees me, her face lights up and she hands me six sheets of unlined paper filled with names, addresses, and telephone numbers in her perfect handwriting

She has numbered the list, and there are sixty-three Bowmans. "So many," she says softly. For a minute I am confused. Then I realize that she is searching for Victoria.

"Wow. Did you copy all these from the telephone book?" I can't believe she looked up so many ZIP codes.

Tina nods. "Now we can write letters," she says.

"But we don't know who all these people are," I say. Tina takes out a letter she has written.

*Dear Mister Mrs. Bowman,*
*   We are looking for our friend, Victoria Bowman.*
*If she is your daughter, please answer.*
                              *Faithfully yours,*
                              *Sarah Wu*
                              *Tina Liang*

Tina is watching my face. "Your letter is good," I say. She smiles.

Naomi comes up behind Tina. "What's all that?" She puts her face close to the paper. "Did Tina write all those addresses?"

I wish she would ask Tina instead of me.

"From the telephone book," Tina says.

"Hey, she does speak English." Naomi starts to read the names and addresses out loud. "Okay, I gotcha," she says. "You guys are trying to find Victoria."

More and more kids are waiting around the door. It smells like wet gym shoes. Rainwater from my short hair is dripping down my neck. Finally Miss Renfro comes with the key and we settle in our seats.

"First to go will be A through G," Miss Renfro says.

"Go where?" I ask.

Naomi holds a pretend camera to her eye. My stomach drops. I completely forgot that it was picture day. That's why everyone is wearing nice clothes. Naomi has on a dark blue turtleneck and a gold chain around her neck. Tina is wearing a dress with a high waist and lace around the collar. I look down at my own T-shirt. Two years ago, Mom took Victoria and Sam and me to a nature camp where we tie-dyed T-shirts. We wore them on the same day and pretended to be triplets. By now the colors have faded so much that you can hardly see the swirl in the middle. Everyone in the room is talking. Miss Renfro taps her ruler on the desk. "Quiet down and start today's journal entry," she says in the low voice she uses when she's getting mad.

Naomi writes a sentence at the top of her paper and shows it to me and Tina: *I have an idea about how we can find Victoria.*

I raise my eyebrows. Tina leans over to see better.

"Let's go to your house after school," Naomi whispers.

"Naomi, no talking," Miss Renfro says. Naomi blushes and puts her notebook back on her desk.

I wonder what Naomi's idea is. I keep looking at her, but she is afraid Miss Renfro will catch her talking again. She turns her notebook to a new page and at the top she writes *CLUES.*

Clues to what? How can we find clues to where Victoria has moved? Tina takes out her small English-Chinese dictionary and looks up "clues." When she finds the word in Chinese, she writes it at the top of her paper in English and Chinese.

Clues. It makes me think of the board game or a detective story. But Victoria is my friend, not a criminal. Miss Renfro is coming down the row. I better start writing, but I can't think of anything to say. *Today is a gloomy day*, I write quickly.

"Miss Renfro?" comes the voice from the intercom. "Is Sarah Wu there?"

Miss Renfro looks at me and holds down the button. "Yes, she is."

"Please send her to the office."

"Will do," says Miss Renfro, nodding at me.

My stomach flips. What happened?

It's strange to walk down the hallway when it's empty. Once I got called to the office because Sam was sick and they couldn't get hold of Mom at work. I sat with him on my lap until the bell rang and school was out. His hair was all wet with sweat and he held on to my sweater like a baby koala bear. I open the heavy wooden door. Mom is sitting in an orange chair holding a bag.

"We forgot all about picture day," she says cheerfully, "so I brought some clothes for you to change into." Mom opens the bag and holds up a plain white blouse and a blue embroidered blouse from one of my relatives in China.

I can't believe Mom came to school just for that. Nobody else's mom comes just to bring clothes for a school picture. I look around the small office. The secretaries are busy. Nobody is watching us. "I think this tie-dyed T-shirt is just fine," I whisper.

"Remember, we send the school pictures of you and Sam to all your relatives. Maybe it would be nice if you wore the Chinese blouse from your great-uncle so he can see that you like it." Mom takes the blouse out of the bag and holds it up. Why should I wear a Chinese blouse?

Once in first grade when I was in a piano recital I wore a red silk outfit from China. Everyone said how I looked like a china doll, but I wanted to look like a regular girl. My fingers were clumsy and I kept losing my place in the song. The silk pants were slippery and finally I just slid off the piano bench.

"What's Sam wearing?"

"I already took him a button-down shirt."

I can imagine Sam sitting for the photographer, so proud in his light blue shirt that's just like Dad's. On the wall of the office is a painting of a little girl dressed in a frilly dress reading on a park bench. I can see my reflection in the glass, the way my hair has dried in clumps. "I don't think I want to have my picture taken," I say.

"Sarah, please," Mom says in a loud whisper. "Why are you making such an issue out of a simple picture?"

Mom is the one making the issue, not me. I don't have any issue at all. The secretary is looking at us. She sees the embroidered blouse. "That's a very pretty blouse," she says. "Is it from Japan?"

"From China," Mom says.

China, Japan, Africa, they're all the same to the secretary. Faraway places with funny-looking people. I fold my arms across my chest. Mom puts the blouse back in the bag and goes toward the door. I want to change my mind and take the Chinese blouse, but Mom is already out the door. I watch her through the glass, small and thin like Sam. I want to run after her and say, *Sorry, Mom, I'll change my shirt*, but my feet are stuck to the brown-and-white tiles on the floor.

"Hurry back to your classroom," the secretary says.

When I go back to Miss Renfro's, she sends me to the gym right away. The photographer is annoyed because he has already started packing up. I sit in front of the screen. The bright lights are warm on my face. I forgot to brush my hair. But the photographer has already waited long enough. "Smile," he says. Why does everyone's picture have to have a huge grin? He clicks the shutter.

Tina and Naomi are waiting for me on the playground. "Hey, Sarah, we were thinking that we could go over to your house after school and figure out what to do about Victoria," says Naomi. "I mean, we can look at all our clues and come up with some sort of a plan." There she goes again with her clues. But her face is serious. "Somehow we've got to find out which Bowman is her. I bet eventually we'll find her—I mean, unless something really bad happened to her."

"I will call Ma Ma," Tina says, heading toward the building. "At five-thirty, she can come to your house."

I follow Tina to the office. She talks to her mom a mile a minute in Chinese. When she hangs up, she is smiling. "Okay," she says.

During math, I keep thinking about what Naomi said. I've been looking for Victoria everywhere I go, but I never really thought that something bad could've happened to her. I mean, what kind of bad thing could happen to a ten-year-old girl and her mother? First they went to Daniel's, and after that I bet they found an apartment that had the kitchen cabinets on the wall. Victoria said her mom never cooked. She never even went to the grocery store because the stove didn't work. They got French fries at McDonald's. I bet they found a cozy apartment with a nice white stove and no broken window shades. I bet that's what happened.

After school, me and Tina wait for Naomi by the gate. Finally she comes running out of the building. "Sorry, I forgot, I have a flute lesson right after school today." She reaches into her book bag. "Here. You guys can have the clues notebook. Let me know if you find anything." She thrusts the notebook into Tina's hands and runs around the corner of the building.

Mom offers Tina play clothes so she won't mess up her nice dress. It looks funny to see her in a pair of my jeans and a regular T-shirt that doesn't say *Gone Fishing?* or *Happy Birthday* like the T-shirts she brought from China.

Tina looks out the window at Victoria's house. Wet leaves are piled in the gutter. A curtain is blowing from inside to outside. "They forgot to close the window," she says. A squirrel is perched on the windowsill. He pokes his head into the house, changes his mind, and scampers off. "We must close the window."

"That's trespassing," I say quickly. "It's against the law."

Tina looks at me blankly. "Only close the window cannot be against the law."

The wind is blowing hard and leaves are swirling through the open window. The whole time Victoria lived next door to me, she never once invited me into her house. Whenever she came out, she opened the front door just enough to fit through, like she didn't even want me to see inside.

"Animals can go into the house," Tina says. "Better to have the window closed for the winter season." She takes out the clues notebook and all the Bowman addresses fall to the floor. I pick them up. How can we ever find out which one is Victoria? "Inside we can find their name," Tina says.

She has a point. Maybe we can find a bill or something with their name and new address. They must have known where they were going before they left. Maybe we can find a match for one of Tina's addresses. If we go inside the house and shut the windows, we can find out where Victoria and her mother went in their maroon car with a few clothes, a lamp, and one kitten.

"Okay. Let's go," I say.

Tina rolls up the jeans that are too long for her, stands up straight, and takes a deep breath. "Yes," she says softly.

First we go to the honeysuckle house. The pile of buckeyes is all wet, but the note is still dry in the plastic bag. "What is that?" asks Tina.

"A note for Victoria. In case she comes while I'm at school."

Tina nods. She sets the notebook down on the stone seat and we head over to Victoria's house. I slip on the wet leaves and grab Tina's arm to catch my balance. She holds on to me and we walk like that over to the side window. "It is too high," says Tina.

"I can boost you," I say, locking my hands together. Tina puts her foot into my hands, pulls herself up by holding my shoulders, and grabs for the windowsill. She is so light, I practically throw her through the window. What if Victoria and her mom come home right now while we're breaking into their house? What if someone else sees us and calls the police?

"Come," Tina whispers to me. With my fingertips I hold on to the bricks that are sticking out and scramble up until I can reach the window ledge. Once I have a grip, Tina grabs my arm. I swing my leg around and I am in.

The kitchen table is covered with wet leaves. Underneath the leaves is a red-and-white-checked tablecloth. I didn't think they would have a tablecloth on the table. I want to shake it out, but it's soaking wet. We hear scampering.

"Must be squirrels," I say.

Tina stiffens.

"They won't hurt us."

"Squirrels can bite," Tina says.

I stamp my foot. "There. Now I scared them away." We hold hands and go carefully up the stairs. A piece of the ceiling has fallen and there is plaster everywhere, even between my teeth. I step onto the landing and stop. What is that noise?

"The wind," says Tina, stepping across the plaster and into the bathroom. The drain of the tub is all rusty.

Tina walks past the toilet and shuts the window. Then she goes to the back bedroom and I go into Victoria's bedroom, the one that faces mine. It's smaller than I thought. A dresser is against the wall with the fronts of the drawers missing. A pair of shorts with yellow ducks is about to fall out, so I stuff it back.

I tiptoe over to the bed. *The Boxcar Children* is open to the page with a silhouette picture of Benny and Violet by the creek. I find a tissue on the floor to mark the place, shut the book, and put it under the bed. Then I kneel on the bed to shut the window, but it's stuck. I put my weight into it, but it won't budge. Tina comes to help me. She pushes on one side and I push on the other. We hear the window weight fall and the window slams shut. The glass pane shatters all over the mattress.

We don't move. If we do, the glass might slide into our knees. A gust of wind blows through the broken window and a shiver runs through my whole body. "We better go," I whisper.

Tina is staring at the jagged edge of glass still stuck to the window frame. "We must clean up," she says, trying to scoot back gently so the glass doesn't shift on the mattress.

I look around the room. Where is a broom? We can't clean up glass with our bare hands. Plaster is everywhere. In the dust are tiny footprints from a squirrel maybe, or a rat. Tina has found a small broom and dustpan and she is trying to sweep the floor, but all it does is stir the dust into a big cloud. She stops, picks an envelope off the floor, and hands it to me.

Suzanne Lamont is the name on the envelope. I read it out loud.

"Victoria's mom?" asks Tina.

"I don't know."

Tina looks surprised. She asks again in case I misunderstood. "Victoria's mother?"

My voice comes out too loud. "I don't know. I hardly know her mother."

Tina goes back to sweeping. Suddenly I am embarrassed about Victoria's house. Tina must think that my friend is a very dirty girl. I want to tell her that really they didn't want the plaster to fall and the windows to crack and the squirrels to come in. I know they didn't mean to. Sometimes things just happen. Tina's pile is getting bigger.

"I think that's clean enough," I say.

"It is not clean," Tina says, still sweeping.

On the shelf above the bed is a small red, white, and green flag that says *France* on it. I bet Victoria's dad gave it to her. Next to it is a glass horse on three legs because one leg is broken. We have a tube of superglue. When Victoria comes back, I can glue the leg back on for her.

On the floor by the bed is a dusty spiral notebook. I pick it up and wipe the dust off the cover. *The Novel*, it says in curly letters. I wonder if Victoria showed it to her mother. That's why she brought it into her house. I stand it up behind the glass horse. Then I decide to take the notebook home and show it to Mom and Sam.

Above the dresser is a paint-by-number picture of a farm with white fences and horses on a hillside. That's where Victoria wants to live someday. She told me she wants to live on a farm with lots of space and clean white fences with big gates. We can run through the gates and climb the trees. The picture is crooked on the wall. I straighten it as best I can and dust off the frame. Tina is trying to pick up the pieces of glass off the mattress.

"Don't do that. You might cut yourself," I warn. "We better go."

Tina keeps putting the pieces of glass into the dustpan.

"We have to go now," I say, enunciating each word.

Finally Tina dumps the glass into her pile of dust and follows me down the stairs.

The kitten is in the kitchen, batting at something. I pick it up and blow off the dust. It's a school picture of Victoria in second grade. Her hair is matted on one side and her dress is stained. She's barely smiling. I put it into the novel notebook.

There is a scratching noise and the sound of little paws. What if the squirrels do try to bite us? A boy in my kindergarten class got bitten by a squirrel and had to get rabies shots. Fourteen shots in his stomach. I grab Tina by the shoulder. "We have to go. The squirrels might be sick."

"Why sick?"

"Come on."

We crouch on the windowsill. I throw the novel notebook down onto the grass. The ground is farther away than I thought. Tina's eyes look scared. One, two, three. I push with my legs and I am down.

Tina is still up there. "I can't," she says.

"Yes, you can. It's not far."

"I'm afraid."

"Come on."

"I can't. I'm afraid."

Tina's voice is shaking. Her lips are pale. What if she won't jump? "Here. I'll catch you." I stretch my arms toward Tina even though I know she's much too big to catch. She sucks in her breath and closes her eyes. And then she is in the leaves next to me, holding on to my shoulders and crying softly into my sweater.

We sit on the seats in the honeysuckle house. Tina is quiet. "I am tired," she says, closing her eyes.

I open the novel notebook and take out the school picture of Victoria. She's smiling a little with her mouth, but her eyes look sad. It's hard to tell what she's thinking. It's hard to tell what she's thinking even when I'm with her sometimes. After we play for a while, I find out. But with a picture, it's stuck the way it is. Once we went to have a family portrait taken. Dad stood behind Mom with his arm around her. Me and Sam were in front. The photographer kept telling me to smile more. Show those teeth, he said. I tried but I couldn't. Sam was happy because Dad was home, but I knew he was taking the 11:00 flight to San Francisco. Give me a real smile, the man said, and I started crying. You can still tell in the picture from my eyes.

"Victoria will come home soon," Tina says softly, touching my arm.

# T I N G

In January, Ba Ba's boss invited us for a late holiday dinner. Ma Ma couldn't decide what to bring. Ba Ba said his boss was interested in Chinese cooking, but Ma Ma thought Chinese food would be too strange for Americans. She wanted to take ice cream, but ice cream in the middle of winter would give everyone a sore throat. Ma Ma consulted Auntie Daisy.

"Americans like Chinese food," Auntie said, "as long as it's not real Chinese food. No frog." Auntie laughed. I'd almost forgotten how much I liked Po Po's frog soup. "Make Chinese American food, like wontons. Everybody likes wontons. I'll help you fold them," she offered.

Auntie filled up our small kitchen as she bustled around adding this and that to the ground pork in the bowl. When the mixture was ready, she and Ma Ma made the dough, stretching it into thin sheets. Then, using chopsticks, they dabbed a little of the meat mixture into the center of a square of dough and folded it shut. Soon the wontons were boiling on the stove and our kitchen smelled a little like Po Po's apartment in Shanghai. Auntie Daisy took out a few wontons and put them into a bowl for me. "You be the taster, Ting. What do you think?" The meat was soft and full of flavor. I finished the bowlful quickly and Auntie gave me some more. "Better taste a lot of them," she said.

"There will be none left for the boss," Ma Ma said.

"We can always make more." Auntie mixed up another batch of dough. Her hands moved quickly, rolling, stretching, folding. When the wontons were done, Ma Ma went to change her clothes. Auntie sat with me at the kitchen table.

"Tina, I want to show you something." She took her wallet out of her purse and showed me a picture of her son, his blond wife, and their chubby boy with dark Chinese eyes but light brown hair.

"He is very cute," I said. "Does he speak Chinese?"

Auntie Daisy shook her head. "Not even his father speaks Chinese. We tried to talk to our sons in Chinese. They understood but they answered in English. They liked baseball, football, American boy things." Auntie closed her wallet and put her hand on my arm. "Now, if we had had a daughter..."

I looked down. I wanted to tell Auntie that I was not the kind of daughter she thought. I was a daughter who broke a crystal vase and played in a dirty dumpster and lied to her teacher, but the words wouldn't come out in Chinese or English. They wouldn't come out at all. I started reading the newspaper that was open on the table.

"Why are you squinting? We better teach you to do

Chinese eye exercises. I taught my sons to do them every morning. And turn on the light when you read. Do you read in the dark, Tina?" Auntie washed her hands and showed me how to rub my temples, my forehead, my eyelids, first gently and then harder. When I was done, everything was even blurrier than before.

"Do them every day, Ting, in the morning and at night."

Ma Ma changed into a Chinese dress that buttoned down the side, with a red jacket. Why couldn't she wear a normal dress like Auntie Daisy, one that was not so tight around the bottom that she could hardly walk? She put her hair up into a small bun. Auntie made the bun over again to make it look fuller. Then Ma Ma wanted to fix my hair into a crown with red rubber bands.

"I don't want a crown," I said quickly.

Ma Ma's face looked hurt. She dropped her hands and the rubber bands fell to the floor. Auntie Daisy came up behind me and looked into the mirror. "How about a ponytail instead," she said. She turned to Ma Ma. "You know, like the American children have it." She pulled my hair up with the brush and into a high ponytail. It looked just right, exactly like Naomi's, only my face was as Chinese as ever. She pulled my thick hair through the rubber band twice and gave the ponytail a quick brush. "Now doesn't that look nice?" she asked Ma Ma.

Ba Ba wore a business suit. Ma Ma told me to wear the new boots Po Po had sent me from China. It was cold and wet outside.

"Do I have to?"

"Of course you have to," Ba Ba said. He looked me over. "Tuck in your shirt, Ting," he said. Finally Auntie looked at the three of us, put the wontons into a big bowl, and said we were ready.

Ba Ba's boss greeted us at the door. He was wearing a red sweater with reindeer on it. Why didn't Ba Ba wear a sweater instead of a black suit? "Liang, come in. So glad you could make it. And Mrs. Liang, so pleased to meet you." He shook Ma Ma's hand. "And this is the young lady I met that first day who told me her daddy could add faster than a calculator. You sure were right, young lady." Then he turned to Ma Ma. "And what's this you brought? Some real Chinese, I hope." He opened the lid just a little. "Could this be homemade wontons? Did I say it right?"

Ma Ma nodded. I wanted to tell Ba Ba's boss that Ba Ba was not Liang but rather Mr. Liang, and that Ma Ma had her own name and she was not a Liang at all. She was a Wang. And that we brought Chinese *food*, not "Chinese," and that it wasn't real Chinese food because we knew they would not like frog. But I just stayed quietly between my parents and sat down at the big dining room table.

Ma Ma and Ba Ba hardly said a word through the whole dinner. I thought of dinners in Shanghai with all of my uncles and aunts and Po Po and Hong and everyone talking and slurping soup at once and the sound of chopsticks scraping the bowls. My stomach was churning and I smelled the old soapy smell.

"Have some ham, Tina," Ba Ba's boss said, putting a thick slice on my plate. How would I ever eat all that? I had trouble cutting the meat. At home Ma Ma cut it into small pieces before she fried it in the big skillet.

The grownups talked about hunting and guns and vacation spots. Ba Ba kept nodding as other people talked. Ma Ma sat stiff and quiet. There were two other kids besides me, a small girl who kept giggling and a boy about my age who played with his Game Boy while we ate.

Ba Ba's boss asked Ma Ma if she knew about jade. Ma Ma looked confused. Jade? I'd heard the word but wasn't sure what it meant. Ma Ma asked me in Chinese, but I shook my head. The boss went to get the jade to show it to Ma Ma. It was a green stone on a necklace. Ma Ma said the necklace was beautiful but she didn't know anything about the stone. He looked so disappointed.

The boss turned to Ba Ba. "So, Liang, did you get that green card yet?"

Ba Ba took a minute to understand the question. "No, no green card."

"It's bound to come soon," the boss said, patting Ba Ba on the back.

Ba Ba smiled.

When we left, the boss handed Ba Ba an envelope and wished him a happy new year. Ba Ba opened the envelope at home, and inside was a crisp fifty-dollar bill. Ba Ba held it up to the light as if it might not be real. Satisfied, he put it into his wallet.

I took the rubber band out of my hair. Putting all my hair into one high ponytail made my scalp sore.

Tomorrow was Sunday. Ma Ma said I would go with her on the bus to clean the big house. But I didn't want to go. Maybe the broken crystal vase was still in the garbage can all wrapped up in the tissues. I wanted to stay home and go out to my mulberry tree. I could tell Ma Ma I had a stomachache. It wouldn't even be a lie. All that ham was churning around.

I tossed and turned in my bed. Ba Ba had a fifty-dollar bill. Maybe I could ask him if I could buy a block of wood to carve. I had tried to use the carving tools on a board I found in the dumpster, but I couldn't get the chisels to work. That wood was too hard. Maybe if I had a soft piece of wood, I could make a buffalo. Or a pig. A pig would be easy. Maybe I could check the prices of blocks of wood at the hardware store. But Ba Ba had already put the fifty-dollar bill into his wallet with his other dollars. He would buy cigarettes after work. That was what he would buy.

When we got to the big house, Ma Ma gave me a sponge and told me to scrub the bathroom. "Even inside the toilet?" I asked.

"Of course," Ma Ma said, handing me a pair of big yellow rubber gloves.

I put them on, but they made it hard to hold the sponge, and water got inside them. I took them off. I washed around the edge of the toilet and scrubbed the tile on the floor. The gloves floated on top of the bucket.

I blew them up so they would be like balloons. But how could I keep the air in? I took rubber bands off my pig-tails and tied the bottoms of the gloves.

"Ting, what kind of help are you? You play when I ask you to work. You go out when I tell you to stay in. What kind of girl are you?"

I looked down. I was done showing everyone how good Chinese children were. Really they weren't good at all. They made up lies about spots on the rug and mud on their jackets. They hid pieces of broken crystal. I was one of those bad Chinese kids. Even in China, there had to be bad kids. The gloves were floating, swollen giant yellow hands. Then I was crying.

"Ting, shhhh, be quiet, Ting, please."

Ma Ma was in her blue cleaning dress, not a clean white nurse's uniform with a small white hat. A blue dress with stains down the front.

"Ting, stop crying right now. Did you hear me?"

I stopped. It was so quiet that we could hear the drip-ping of the tap in the bathtub. "Ma Ma, I broke the vase," I said. "The crystal vase on the shelf downstairs."

"What are you saying?"

"Ma Ma, you know when I came here with you before, I broke the crystal vase on the shelf."

"And you didn't tell anybody?" Ma Ma's voice was dry. "What happened to you that you don't tell the truth?"

My snot was flowing from my nose into the bucket. Then Ma Ma's hands were on my back, up and down, rough on my skin. She put a cold washcloth on my forehead. I glanced into the mirror. My eyes were red and puffy.

"We will go together and tell the lady," Ma Ma said.

"I'll tell her myself," I whispered.

I went down the stairs slowly. Where was the lady in this big house? She could be in the study or the exercise room or the library or the basement. Finally I found her on the deck outside, in her coat, smoking a cigarette. As soon as she saw me, she put the cigarette behind her back.

"Miss, I want to tell you. Last time I came here, I broke the crystal vase. I'm so sorry. I will pay for the vase."

The lady waved her cigarette. "That vase in the living room? That was something my husband picked up somewhere."

"But I can—"

The lady dropped the cigarette and stamped it out with her shoe. "Don't even worry about it. Now, how's your family been doing?"

"Fine."

"Good. Now we better go inside before we freeze."

I didn't want to go into a house full of things that nobody even wanted. Why did Ma Ma have to dust all those things if the lady didn't care about them? I could take the sculptures carefully off the shelf, pack them up in a box, and sell them. With the tools Uncle sent me, I could carve more animals to sell. Then we would have money for Uncle's plane ticket.

The lady was motioning to me. I followed her into the house.

Miss Renfro said that before we started class, there

would be vision screening in the lunchroom. We had to line up in alphabetical order.

I tried to do Auntie's eye exercises real fast while I waited for my turn. The boy ahead of me could read even the tiniest row of letters. "Twenty twenty," the lady said. "Next."

I stood with my toes touching the white line and squinted at the letters. I could read the first row pretty easily, but after that, I had trouble.

"I can't tell," I said.

"Keep trying," the lady said.

"Sorry, I can't see them," I said.

"You must see something. Do your best."

"A, Z, G, Y, O," I said, choosing random letters.

"Twenty eighty," the lady said, giving me a certificate for free glasses and a letter to my parents saying that I had failed the vision screening. She leaned over and whispered something to the other tester. "Some parents...," the tester whispered back, looking at me.

*Some parents.* What did that mean? That I had some parents? That some parents were better than mine? I wanted to tell the lady that yes, I had some parents, Mrs. Lin Wang and Mr. Zhen Rei Liang, to be exact, and that they were fine, just fine parents.

When Ma Ma saw the letter that afternoon, she said that glasses were a crutch and that they would make my eyes even worse. "Just do Auntie's eye exercises, Ting." She put the letter on the kitchen counter.

"Eye exercises help, but not sixty points," Auntie

Daisy said. She looked at the coupon. "The glasses are free with this paper. Let's go to the mall and see."

At the eyeglasses store, Auntie did all the talking. The lady showed us the free frames. They were thick plastic and very round. I picked up some smaller wire-rimmed ones that cost forty dollars. I looked sophisticated when I tried them on, like a teacher or a scientist.

"No, Ting," Ma Ma said. "These are the free frames. You want pink or blue?" She was talking loudly in Chinese. The optician ladies were looking at each other. Ma Ma stuck the pink pair on my face. "What do you think?" she asked Auntie.

"I don't know," Auntie said, adjusting them on my nose.

"We take pink one," Ma Ma said, handing the lady my prescription.

I would never wear the glasses. They couldn't make me. I walked fast, away from Ma Ma and Auntie and right to the hardware store. Everything in the window was on sale. I saw some wood in thin sheets called balsa wood. If I had that kind of wood, I could make model airplanes that really flew. I could make a 747 with a long thin tail, the kind that Uncle would take when he came to visit.

"Ting," Ma Ma said loudly. Why couldn't she call me Tina when we were in the shopping mall? I looked around. "Ting, what are you looking at? We are going to the drugstore now to wait for your glasses. Come."

When I put the new glasses on, Ma Ma's face was all wrinkled like Po Po's. Auntie Daisy's too. The leaves on the trees were just starting to bud, so tiny and perfect. I looked down at my feet. I was taller than I thought.

When we got home, Ma Ma showed Auntie the catalog for the nursing college. Auntie looked it over. "It is a very good program," she said. "And it takes only two years."

"First I have to convince my husband," Ma Ma said.

With my glasses on, the whole apartment was spinning.

That night I lay in my bed and tried to sleep, but Ma Ma and Ba Ba were shouting so loud in the other room. Something about jobs and money. Ba Ba said they had to save more money first. They could move anywhere. Chicago was a big city with lots of jobs and big houses to clean. Ba Ba wanted to go there or to New York.

"I don't want to clean more houses. I want to study," Ma Ma shouted.

"You want to be a nurse but you don't know English yet."

"That's why I am taking English classes."

"First you want English classes. Okay. But now you want to study nursing for two years? And how can we pay for all this?" Ba Ba shouted. "You want everything right now." Ba Ba banged on the table. "You cannot wait."

"I have been waiting all my life," Ma Ma said, "and now I am done waiting."

"How can you say you are done waiting when we still don't have the green card."

"The letter said—"

Ba Ba hit the table. "The letter said this or the letter said that. Still the green card is not here. Who knows? It may never arrive. My friend waited for two years and then they said no, no green card for you."

"There must have been some reason. He must have been involved—"

"Involved in nothing. No. They had enough Chinese. That's all."

Ma Ma was crying. *Some parents.* Some parents who shouted so loud all the neighbors could hear. Some parents who banged on the table.

I covered my head with the blanket. The air was warm and steamy. I would earn money myself so I could buy the balsa wood. Sarah said her mother was good at making things. Maybe she knew how to carve wood. Sarah's mother could teach me. She taught Sarah so many things. Sam too. They knew all about plants and cooking. They read library books. I would start by carving simple shapes. Someday I would carve beautiful animals that people would buy. You didn't need a green card to sell animals.

When I woke up, the apartment was quiet. I put on my glasses and tiptoed out to the kitchen to get a drink. Ba Ba's wallet was on the kitchen table. I opened it up. The fifty-dollar bill was gone. In its place was a five-dollar bill and four ones. What did Ba Ba buy with the rest? A kung fu video? Cigarettes? Next to the money was a business card from a lawyer in Chicago. What if the lawyer couldn't help Ba Ba get the green card? Then would we go back to China? But there was opportunity in America. Ma Ma would become a nurse. We could save money to buy a little house. And by now I forgot how to write so many Chinese characters. What would my teacher say when she saw my writing full of mistakes?

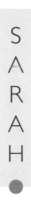

SARAH

There's something hitting my window. I glance at the clock. Two o'clock in the morning. Outside the locust tree is bending and hailstones are pinging off the window pane. I cup my hands around my eyes and look over to Victoria's. Her bed must be covered with hailstones. I should have put *The Boxcar Children* somewhere better than just under the bed. It will get wet there when the hailstones melt.

I turn on my light, take the novel notebook out from under my bed, and trace the fancy letters on the cover. The little island picture under the title has faded, but you can still see the palm trees with their coconuts. Victoria is good at drawing. Maybe someday she'll be an artist. We can make books together. I hold the photo of her close to the light. You can even see the blue veins in her forehead. I put the photo in the pocket of my pajamas, turn the light off, and lie down. Lightning fills up my room and thunder shakes the whole house.

Sam is in the doorway. "Sarah, can I sleep with you?"

Before I have time to answer, Sam is under my covers with his teeth chattering. He's trying to tell me that he's scared.

"Shhh, Sam." I rub his back for a long time, up and down and up and down. Finally I can feel the muscles relax. The thunder crashes and he tenses up again. "It's okay, Sam. It's just a spring storm." I rub his back some more.

"S-S-Sarah?"

"Hmm?"

"Can you tell me a story?"

When Sam was little, we shared a room. Every night when Mom and Dad thought we were asleep I made up stories for him. Mostly they were about a beaver family that had a home in our basement. They had four little beavers, Mini, Waddie, Wheeze, and Up.

"One day, Wheeze fell asleep in the dryer," I start. "Mother Beaver came down to do the laundry. She put in Mini's tie-dyed T-shirt, Waddie's blue jeans, Wheeze's baseball cap, and Up's socks, but she never noticed Wheeze."

"And Father's shorts," Sam whispers.

"And Father's shorts."

I can feel Sam's muscles get soft. Even when the thunder crashes, his breathing is slow and even. No need to finish the story. Sam is asleep. With his eyes closed, he looks like a newborn mouse. I'm not sure, anyway, how my story would have gone. Would Wheeze have scampered out of the dryer? Dryers get so hot, he could have been burned. He could even have died. But my stories for Sam always ended happily.

Hailstones as big as golf balls are hitting my window. The locust tree is bending so far that I think it will break. Branches of the hackberry are hitting the roof. A huge limb falls off the oak, taking Victoria's gutter on its way down. The storm sirens sound.

"Sarah, Sam, head to the basement," Mom shouts.

"Sam!" I shake him but he's so sleepy that he hardly moves. "Sam, there's a tornado or something." Sam opens his eyes for a minute, but he won't get up. I put my arms around him and half carry, half drag him along the hallway to the top of the stairs.

"Set him on his feet," Mom says. With Mom on one side and me on the other, we carry Sam down both flights of stairs to the small rug by the washing machine, where he curls up like a kitten. Mom picks up an old blanket and covers him.

"What about Victoria's kitten?" I ask.

Mom goes to the window and cups her hands around her eyes. "I don't see him. You know, I bet he found a safe place to hide. Animals are good at that."

"Even baby ones?"

"He's not so little anymore."

Mom and I sit on the old sofa by the dryer. Outside the small window the rain is white. Mom strokes my short hair over and over. Her hand feels good on my scalp. She looks at the clock above the washing machine and at her wristwatch too. I know she's wondering about Dad. I should tell her not to worry, he will be home soon. But how do I know? What happens to airplanes when there's lightning all around?

Thunder shakes our house like an earthquake. I push my face into Mom's shoulder and cover my ears. I can feel the lightning even with my eyes closed. Sometimes me and Victoria pretend we are blind. We lead each other blindfolded around the back yard, but we can always tell if we are in the light or the shade. A real blind person can't feel the light except where it's warm. Over and over Mom's rough hand is in my hair.

Sam moves a little on the rug and mumbles something.

"What did he say?" I ask.

"Sarah."

"Are you sure?"

"Positive."

Mom pulls a blanket over our backs and wraps it around my shoulders so we're in a cocoon. She keeps looking at the clock.

"I bet the airport was closed," I whisper.

After a while the thunder is farther away. It's still raining, but the lightning is not as bright.

"You kids had better get some sleep," Mom says. "It's after three."

"Sam is sleeping," I say.

"What about you?"

"I'm not tired."

Sam smiles in his sleep and moves his arm up over his head. What's he dreaming about? The little beavers? Tossing the football? Getting in D?

"Did I look like Sam when I was little?" I ask.

"A little. But he looks more like Dad."

"Do I look like you?"

"It's hard to say."

Mom takes an old photo album off the shelf above the washer. I think I've looked at it before, but it's been so long I hardly remember. The first page has a photo of a little girl with straight bangs. "Is that you?" I ask.

Mom nods. "After my first haircut." I look closely at the face. The lips are thin and curved like mine. "I remember I was mad because I wanted to keep my long hair."

"Why did you cut it?"

"My mom made me. She said long hair was too much trouble."

I look closely at my grandmother. Her face is stern. "You don't look like your mother."

"More like my father, people say."

We find a picture of my grandfather. He has the same dark eyes as Mom and the same softness to his face. Mom holds the album up next to me. "I'd say you look a little like my father too."

We go through the whole album. There is a picture of Mom in a school play wearing a clown costume. Except for Mom, all the kids are white.

"Was it weird to be the only Asian kid in your class?"

"Sometimes."

"Now I'm not the only one since Tina came."

"That must be nice."

I think for a minute. "Sometimes it is, sometimes it isn't."

"I always wished there were another Chinese girl in my class. There was for a short time, but she moved away," Mom says.

We close the photo album. "I found an old picture of Victoria," I say, taking it out of my pajama pocket.

Mom holds the photo closer to the window. Then she gets up, rummages around in the storage closet, and comes back with a small wooden picture frame. "Would you like to put Victoria's picture in here?" She dusts the glass off with her finger.

The picture fits perfectly into the frame.

"Where do you think Victoria and her mother are?" I ask Mom.

Mom is playing with my hair. "Do you know if they have any family nearby?"

"She has a cousin somewhere around here."

"Maybe they went there."

"Do you think something could have happened to them?"

Mom stops moving her fingers. "You know, Sarah, something could happen to any of us every day. Something good or something bad."

"Sometimes we don't even know if it's good or bad," I say.

The kitten is at the basement window, meowing.

"Can I let him in?"

Mom sighs. "I never wanted a pet." He meows again. "But go ahead."

I open the door and the kitten comes in. He sniffs Sam on the floor, then jumps onto my lap and lies down. I pet him under his neck and feel the low purr in my stomach. Good things happen and bad things and medium things. When Victoria left, it was a bad thing. But maybe it was good for her. I don't know. Then Tina came. That is a good thing for me. For her, I don't know. She's with her mom, but she misses her uncle and her grandmother. The storm was bad because Dad isn't home and it broke the gutter off Victoria's roof. But it was good because me and Mom and Sam spent the night in the basement and now we have let the kitten into the house.

The sun is just starting to rise, and pink light is on Mom's face. Sam stretches and opens his eyes. When he sees the kitten on my lap, he smiles. Mom lets me take the kitten upstairs to my bed.

When I wake up, the room is washed in light. I look out the window. There are twigs and branches everywhere. Dad's car is not in the driveway. My stomach drops.

Mom is downstairs dozing on the sofa with a book open on her lap. Her head is back and the veins in her neck pop out. I want to move her into a more comfortable position, but that might wake her up. I tiptoe over to the closet, slip on my shoes, put my jacket on over my pajamas, and head out.

The temperature must have dropped thirty degrees, and the wind blows right through my pajama pants. The sky is a brilliant blue. The limb of Victoria's oak is in the driveway, and the gutter is in her front yard. I step over all the branches to get closer. The tiny oak sapling is still there with its bright green leaves. Where would be a good place to plant an oak? I walk around to the back yard. It would be nice to have an oak tree by the entrance of the honeysuckle house, surrounded by yellow and white daffodils. The soil is soaking wet. I make a hole with a stick. Then I remember the bone meal. If it's good for bulbs, it's probably good for trees. I take the bag off the porch and dump a handful into the hole. I take the sapling out of the gutter, careful not to knock off the acorn clinging to its roots, put it into the hole and pat the soil firmly around the tiny trunk. Victoria will like having an oak tree for shade in the summer.

The kitten comes over and rubs against my jacket. I wonder where he hid during the storm. Under the porch, maybe. He settles himself against the sapling. "Move over," I tell him, but he shuts his eyes in the sun and purrs. "Come on, kitty, be careful. It's only a baby." I push him away from the tiny oak tree.

A car is coming slowly up the street. I can hear the tires crunching the twigs. Maybe Victoria and her mother are coming back to see if their house is okay. Even if they moved, it's still their house. The crunching stops and the motor dies, but I don't hear a car door opening. I turn around. There is a fancy blue Saab parked in front of Victoria's house. The windows are tinted, so I can't see anyone inside. Nobody gets out of the car.

A gust of wind whips around our carport. I stand up, run in through the back door, and watch out the window. Ten minutes go by, but still nobody gets out of the car. My stomach is so empty it hurts. I pour myself a bowl of cereal and eat it slowly by the window. I am just about ready to go up and get dressed when a maroon Toyota pulls up next to the Saab. The door of the Toyota opens, and Victoria slips into the blue car. Before the door is even closed, the car screeches its wheels and speeds down the street. The Toyota follows slowly and turns left at the corner.

The cereal is like a ball in my stomach. Who took Victoria? What if they never come back? Maybe the blue Saab was Daniel's car. Or maybe her dad came back from France and bought a blue Saab. I set my bowl of half-eaten cereal in the sink and take a deep breath. I could have run out real quick and asked Victoria where she was going. Instead I sat there eating.

The telephone rings. Mom and Sam are both asleep. I swallow hard and run to get it before it rings again.

"Sarah, it's Dad."

I can hardly talk.

"Are you okay?" he asks.

"Yes. Fine."

"Listen, I was stuck in the plane for several hours and it finally landed in Atlanta. I should be home around six o'clock tonight."

"Okay."

"Is Mom there?"

"She's asleep."

"Okay. See you soon."

Dad is waiting for me to say something else. Something like *I'm glad you called*, or *I missed you*, or *I can't wait to see you*, but no words come out.

"I missed you," Dad says.

Words are easy for him. He makes speeches at business meetings. He tells his employees what to do. He smiles with all his teeth.

"Okay, bye." It comes out like a whisper.

The whole neighborhood is out looking at the storm damage. One man had a branch come right through his roof. Dewayne says their garage folded onto their car. Naomi's mother walks up the hill to our front yard. "We were lucky," she tells Mom. "No real damage, just a scratch on the car." They look over at Victoria's. "Lucky they lost only a gutter. You know, Naomi tells me they disappeared."

"We haven't seen them for a while," Mom says. "But now I see that the windows are closed. They must've come and shut them because they were open last week."

"Unless someone else shut them," Naomi's mom says. "You know, anyone could be wandering around in an empty house like that."

My stomach flips over. What if somebody saw me and Tina go into Victoria's house?

"Hey, let's go around back," Naomi says, motioning for me to follow her. When we get to the honeysuckle house, she asks if me and Tina added anything to the clues notebook.

"Nope."

Naomi sighs. "So you guys didn't find any new clues?" I don't want to tell Naomi about the broken window or the blue car. She'll put her hand to her mouth and say that Victoria's been kidnapped.

"Not really," I say, controlling my voice.

"Tina told me you found a picture of Victoria. Did you put it into the notebook?"

"No."

"Why not?"

I could just say that I lost it. Or it didn't fit. "Because it's not a clue. It's a picture of my friend," I say slowly.

"You act like everyone who's your friend isn't anyone else's friend," Naomi says, closing the notebook and tucking it under her arm. She looks like she's going to cry. I don't know what to do. I should be nice, but I don't feel like it. Mom is in the side yard gathering branches. I want to go out of the honeysuckle house, but I can't just leave Naomi. The pile of buckeyes is still there, and the plastic bag with the note too. I pull it up a little, and then I see that the note inside the bag is not the one I wrote. When did Victoria put it there? I don't want Naomi to see the note. Another clue, she'll say. She'll want to tape it into the notebook.

We are both quiet. I show Naomi the buckeye game that Tina taught me so we'll have something to do.

Naomi's mother calls her. As soon as she's gone, I open the plastic bag and unfold the note.

*Dear Sarah,*
   *Thanks for the letter. I like the Chinese writing.*
                          *Love,*
                          *Victoria*
   *P.S. I have two stepsisters from France.*

Victoria copied the Chinese characters for *peng you* along the bottom of the letter. She must have practiced first. The characters are dark and even. I read the letter over and over. I can't tell if Victoria is sad or happy. She always wished she had a sister, an orphan sister. Maybe her stepsisters like to pretend. But maybe they are still in France. I go inside and write a letter back to Victoria.

> *Dear Victoria.*
> *Where are you living now? My friend Tina taught me the Chinese writing. I hope to see you soon.*
> > *Your friend,*
> > *Sarah*

When I read over what I've written, I don't like it. Victoria might not want to tell me where her apartment is. She might not want me to visit. She never wanted me to come into her house. The part about Tina bothers me too. I throw the letter away and write a new one.

> *Dear Victoria,*
> *I wish we could still play. Maybe next time you come, I'll be home. Do your stepsisters like to play orphan?*
> > *Your friend,*
> > *Sarah*

I put the letter in the plastic bag and take it out to the buckeye pile. I sit for a while on my stone. Maybe

Daniel took Victoria shopping in the blue car. Maybe her dad is taking her to visit a farm. She'd like that. Sam and Dewayne are tossing a tennis ball back and forth. Dad pulls into the driveway. Sam is jumping around telling Dad all about the storm. What does he know? He was asleep through the whole thing.

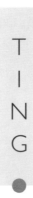

T
I
N
G

Ma Ma asked me to help her with her English home-work. She was supposed to make up ten sentences about herself. I put my glasses on so I could see more clearly. Her first sentence was *My daughter is name Tina.* *Named*, I corrected. The next one was *My daughter is very good girl.*

"You have to put in the *a*," I said, adding it with a red pen.

Ma Ma nodded.

The third sentence said *I am from the China.*

"You don't say *the* China."

"It is true. I am from the China."

"I am from China," I corrected.

Ma Ma sighed. "English is so complicated. Maybe I am too old to learn."

I looked at Ma Ma's forehead with its deep lines and I wondered if maybe she was right.

While Ma Ma was doing her homework, I took my

carving tools out back and whittled a small branch that was on the ground by the dumpster. It was easy to get the outer bark off. But what could I make out of just a branch? Suddenly I had an idea. When I was at Sarah's house the other day, Sam was trying so hard to whistle. He puckered his lips and blew, but he could not make a whistling sound. I would make him a whistle.

The middle of my stick was soft, so I poked a thinner stick into it to hollow it out. Using the carving knife, I cut a hole near the top of the branch. Then I blew, but no sound came out. I used the chisel to make the edge of the hole thinner. Still the air would not whistle. It was coming out of the bottom too fast. I found a thin stick and whittled it down until it fit into the bottom of the whistle, and then I blew again. Out came a clear low sound. Sam would like that. He would run all over their back yard blowing his whistle.

I wrote a letter to tell Uncle that I used the tools to make a real whistle. *The sound is beautiful*, I wrote. *I wish you could hear it. Maybe if I blow it loud enough.* I took the whistle out of my pocket and blew as hard as I could.

"Ting, please don't make so much noise. I am studying," Ma Ma said.

I tried to finish my letter, but I forgot the Chinese character for "carve". If I asked Ma Ma, she would tell me not to interrupt her while she was studying. I couldn't remember the order of the strokes. I balled up my letter and tossed it into the garbage can.

•

Ba Ba went to Chicago for a few days and came back with a new VCR and two kung fu movies but no green card. He started watching the first movie right away. Ma Ma cooked pork and bean threads, but he barely looked up to eat. Ma Ma and I sat at the kitchen table and ate by ourselves while he watched.

"Look," Ba Ba said. I glanced over. One man was flipping another over his head. Ba Ba moved closer to the screen. Ma Ma wouldn't look.

"What's the matter?" Ba Ba asked. His voice was angry. "You think you are the only one who can spend money?"

Ma Ma didn't answer.

Ba Ba shook his head. The men on the screen were shouting, so Ba Ba talked very loud. He lit a cigarette and turned back to the screen. I felt the bean threads coming back into my throat, choking me. I ran into my room and flung myself onto my bed.

It got quiet. Ba Ba must have turned off the television. He was coming into my room. I didn't look up, but I knew he was standing in the doorway. For a minute I saw Ba Ba in China. He smoked outside in front of our building with Uncle and Mr. Liu. They laughed and talked and ate noodles.

Ba Ba sat still on the edge of my bed. He didn't say anything. Ma Ma came into the room too. We were all there together. Ma Ma's soft footsteps came closer to the bed. Ba Ba moved over and Ma Ma sat next to him. A hand was on my head. Ma Ma's hand or Ba Ba's, I wasn't sure. They were straightening the covers, pulling them up on my back so I would not get cold.

It was dark when I woke up. Ma Ma was still there on the bed. She said I was such a good girl. She was so proud of me. "Come, Ting. We'll clean up the dishes."

Ba Ba was watching the picture on television with no sound. I dried the dishes that Ma Ma washed and stacked them neatly on the shelf. When the table was all cleaned off, I watched the strong men on the television doing kung fu. One was a lady. Their movements were crisp and clear. They shouted and kicked and punched. When the movie was over, Ba Ba stood up and started kicking like the men on the screen, front, back, side. His leg was so high he almost hit the lamp. He stood with his knees bent, breathing hard.

I went into my room, bent my knees, and took a deep breath. I tried to kick my leg, but I almost fell. I tried again. This time I put my hand on my stomach. I had to breathe more evenly. Over and over I bent my legs and tried to stand as still as I could. Some day I would do it perfectly. Ba Ba would be so proud. He would write Uncle and tell him that I was learning kung fu. When the girls made their eyes long at me or grabbed for the bunny on my jacket, I would breathe from my stomach, bend my knees, and kick.

The next morning my legs were so sore that I could hardly walk. "What's wrong?" Ba Ba asked when he saw me limp into the kitchen.

"My legs are very sore," I said.

"Why?"

"From practicing kung fu." I showed Ba Ba how I stood with my legs bent. They hurt so much I could hold the position for only a second.

"Very good, Ting. The more you practice, the less your legs will hurt." Ba Ba set out two bowls of noodles for breakfast.

"Is Ma Ma still asleep?" I asked.

"She is very tired," Ba Ba said.

"But she never sleeps late."

Ba Ba cleared his throat. "The baby makes her tired," he said softly.

"The baby?"

Ba Ba looked down at his noodles. "We are going to have another baby, Ting."

How could Ma Ma have a baby in her small stomach? Ma Ma was too old to have a baby. I was already ten. Nobody else who was ten years old had a baby sister or brother. Ba Ba must be joking.

"Are you happy, Ting?" Ba Ba asked. I looked hard at his face. His jaw was square and set. His eyes were not joking at all. "The baby will be the first real American in our family. A real American baby." Ba Ba was holding his chopsticks. "Now Immigration will say yes, they have an American baby. They have to stay in America."

But I was a real American too. My English was almost perfect. I was Ma Ma and Ba Ba's baby. That's what Po Po always said when we were in China. Don't forget, you are Ma Ma and Ba Ba's baby and soon you will see them in America. But Po Po didn't tell me about the soap smell and Ching Chang Chung and the girls who clawed at my bunny.

Ba Ba pushed back his bowl and stood up. "Come, Ting, today we will practice punching." He showed me how to stand in the horse position and throw my fist forward. My legs hurt but I didn't stop. Over and over we practiced until the punch felt just right. "Very good, Ting," Ba Ba said.

Ma Ma came out of the bedroom.

"Did you see, Ma Ma?" Ba Ba asked. "Ting has very good balance."

"I saw," Ma Ma said with the sleep still on her face. "Very good."

My eyes went to Ma Ma's stomach.

She looked at Ba Ba. "I told her," he said.

"It is still very small, Ting," she whispered. "You cannot see."

I nodded.

"It will be born in summer."

"I wonder if it's a boy or a girl."

"Auntie Daisy says a boy. She says it's small and a small baby is a boy."

"She already knows about our baby?"

Ma Ma nodded.

"Why didn't you tell me before?"

"Now we told you, Ting," Ma Ma said. "Now is the time."

## S A R A H

When I walk home after school, Dad's car is in the driveway. He must be sick. Otherwise, why would he be home in the middle of the day? He is in Victoria's yard, picking up branches. "What are you doing?" I ask when I get close.

"Cleaning up."

There must be some reason Dad is home. He never takes days off for nothing. Once when I was in kindergarten, he picked me up from school because Mom had the flu. I got scared when I saw him by the coat rack with all the moms.

Dad asks me to help him move the gutter into Victoria's garage. Then we tie the branches into bundles with string and put them by the curb. He looks up at the abandoned house. "Strange, isn't it," he says, "the way they just disappeared."

I don't say anything. "Disappeared" makes it sound like they vanished into thin air. They left, that's all. And they've been coming back, only we haven't had a chance to see them. Anyway, lots of things are strange, like the way he stayed home today for no reason at all and now he's cleaning up Victoria's yard.

"Sarah, can you put your finger on this knot for me?"

Dad pulls the twine and I hold the knot while he ties it again. I can't stand it any longer, so finally I just come straight out and ask, "Why are you home in the middle of the day?"

Dad ties a triple knot. "I was tired after spending hours in an airplane, going from one airport to the next." He stops talking and looks at the sky. I know he's trying to find the words. "Then when we finally landed and I was driving home, I saw trees uprooted all over the place and a trailer turned upside down."

I wonder what all this has to do with staying home today. I break a stick into smaller and smaller pieces.

"All I could think of was how much I wanted to get home and see all of you. So I took a day off."

"You mean Sam," I say. I didn't mean to say it. I want to take the words back, but it's too late. Dad is trying to find every stick in the yard. He has a bundle of little sticks too small to tie. He drops them all and grabs me by the shoulders. He's going to shake me because I should never say things like that to my father.

"All of you," he whispers.

He looks at the ground. I wish he would spank me like he did when I was little. I don't remember what I did, but he spanked me. Not hard, just with his hand. If he spanks me I'll cry, but now no tears come.

Dad is sweaty like he gets from hot Chinese food. I can tell he's trying to say more, but the words are stuck like when I wanted to tell Mom that I really would wear the Chinese blouse.

"I thought we should help clean up your friend's house. Help out a little," Dad says.

"Her name's Victoria."

"Victoria's house." He looks up at the broken window. "Guess the hail did it," he says, pointing.

"No, it didn't."

"Oh, no?"

"I broke it. With Tina. You don't even know Tina, do you?" The words come out without stopping. "We went in to see if we could figure out where Victoria went and shut their windows so the rain wouldn't go in and the leaves and squirrels and everything. The window was stuck so Tina helped me, and it crashed down and shattered all over the bed."

Dad's arms are hanging limp at his sides and the ball of twine is unraveled on the ground. "It was nice of you to shut their windows," he says finally. "When they come back, we'll offer to replace the glass."

I wait for Dad to say something about the danger of going into abandoned buildings and how it's against the law, but he is picking up sticks again. He opens his mouth and closes it. I wait.

"You know, maybe we could try to find out where they moved to. We can see if they have a new address listed with the phone company," he says finally.

"What if they don't?"

"We can try the courthouse."

"What if they aren't listed there either?"

Dad is thinking. "Then I don't know," he says.

I wander into the honeysuckle house. My note is still there in the plastic bag. The buckeyes aren't shiny and warm anymore. I pick one up, and mold is growing on the underside. I rub it off with my thumb. I pick up another one, and it has split near the bottom. Inside is a small green shoot. I'll plant it out front so we can have a buckeye tree to shade the house.

The sun is making spots on my legs as it shines through the branches. I look up. Our honeysuckle house has small green leaves. A bird's nest is in the ceiling. When the leaves were big, we never noticed it, but now it is clear against the sky.

Miss Renfro is handing out big envelopes. My stomach drops. School pictures. Miss Renfro says that if our parents are not pleased with the pictures we can go for a retake after spring break. That's what I'll do. I'll go for a retake with the Chinese blouse. Then Mom can send the wallet-size pictures to my great-uncles in China.

Miss Renfro goes around the class looking at each photo through the oval cellophane-covered hole. I don't even want to look at mine, but Miss Renfro says what a nice picture it is, so I have to look. Actually, it's not that bad. Just a little of the tie-dyed T-shirt shows.

Most of the kids in the class are trading pictures. Tina asks if she can have a small picture of me to send to Mu

Ying. "She can see my new friend," she says. I cut out one wallet-size photo and we trade. Tina has her two pigtails hanging perfectly on either side of her head. For a minute I think I can show Victoria, but then I don't know when I'll see her. I put the picture of Tina in the big envelope so it won't get dirty or creased.

Tina is looking at her eight-by-ten. "This one is very big," she says. "I will send this one to my grandmother in China." Then she takes out the three-by-five. "And this one is for Ba Ba."

"For who?" I ask.

She looks at me, surprised. "Ba Ba." Then she claps her hand over her mouth. "I forgot, you don't speak Chinese. This one is for my father. He can look at this picture of me when he is in Chicago."

"Chicago?"

"He goes there to see the immigration lawyer."

"Who?"

"The lawyer who will help him get the green card so he can work in America."

"How long does he stay in Chicago?"

"Sometimes three or four days. Sometimes one month."

"And you and your mom stay in Cincinnati?"

"Yes. Ma Ma doesn't like Chicago."

I never knew Tina's dad wasn't with her all the time. She puts the picture back in the envelope.

Naomi says her picture is awful.

"Can I see?" Tina asks.

Slowly she takes it out of the envelope. Her eyes are

not open wide, but other than that, it's fine.

"I don't see why you don't like it," I say. "I don't think it's so bad."

"I have Chinese eyes," Naomi says.

She doesn't notice what she said. Tina doesn't either. They just go on talking.

"What's wrong with Chinese eyes?" My voice comes out loud. Naomi puts her hand over her mouth. Tina is not following. "Chinese eyes are just fine," I say slowly.

Naomi looks like she might cry. It will be my fault. I know I should look away, but I won't take my eyes off of Naomi's bright blue ones.

"I didn't mean anything," she whispers.

Before going into my house, I stop in the honeysuckle house. The plastic bag is under a rock on my seat. I open it carefully. Inside is a piece of blue paper. A school photo falls out when I unfold the note.

> *Dear Sarah,*
>
> *Here is my new school picture. My stepsisters are Charlotte and Dominique. When I see you, we can play barge. You are the barge man and I am the daughter who helps shovel the coal. Or do you want to be the daughter? Sam can be the brother if he wants.*
>
> 
>
> *Love,*
> *Victoria*
>
> 

I look closely at the picture. Victoria's hair is all combed out and she has the barrette I once gave her on the side. She is smiling. On the back it says, *To my friend Sarah, love Victoria.*

I sweep the leaves around the entryway into a pile. Small green shoots are sticking up through the dirt underneath. They must be the bulbs we planted back in November. I spread the leaves over the shoots again like a blanket. The kitten stretches and rubs against my jacket. His fur gets stuck to the sleeve. I sit back on my rock seat and the kitten settles on my lap. He opens and closes his claws in my jeans. He is so big now, he stretches from one of my knees to the other. I pet the soft fur on his neck and feel him purr.

I wonder what a barge man does. What would it be like to be the daughter of a man who went up and down the river all day? I would worry about whirlpools in the icy water. What if one day my dad fell in?

I glance toward my house. I can see Mom through the window stirring something on the stove. Sam is talking to her, but I can't hear the words. It's like I'm watching television with the sound off. I bet he's asking her when Dad's coming home. He's asking her exactly which way the plane is going.

I look at the photo of Victoria more closely. Her eyes are not red around the edges. Her mouth is smiling a little. If something bad had happened, I think I could tell. Somehow I could.

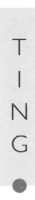

T
I
N
G

**When I got to school, Sarah was by the fence reading as** usual. "I borrowed a book from the library about whittling wood," she said when I got close. "I thought maybe it'd help you figure out how to use the carving tools, I mean until your uncle comes."

I couldn't believe that Sarah had picked out a book especially for me. We looked at the table of contents together. The first project was a slingshot and the second was an Indian bow. "I made a whistle the other day," I said.

"Does it really work?"

"Yes. I made it for Sam."

Sarah smiled. "He'll be so happy. He keeps trying to whistle, but he just can't get the sound to come out."

After school we walked to my apartment to pick up the carving tools. I put the wooden whistle for Sam in my book bag. We got a drink of water and rested in my living room for a few minutes before heading over to Sarah's. I wanted to walk on the big street the way I usually went with Ma Ma, but Sarah knew a shortcut.

"Is it trespassing?" I asked.

"I guess so. But I think it's okay," Sarah said. "Sam goes that way to Dewayne's all the time."

We went past the dumpster in back of my apartment. "Sometimes I find good things in there," I told Sarah.

"Really? Like what?"

"Once I found some nails."

"Lucky. I wish we had a dumpster like that."

"But sometimes it's full of bees and smelly garbage."

We cut over to the yard behind ours and crossed the street. On the way we saw yellow flowers blooming everywhere. "They're crocuses," Sarah said.

"Crocuses," I repeated.

"And these are daffodils." She pointed to green leaves sticking out of the ground. "They'll bloom in a couple of weeks."

"You know so much about flowers."

Sarah shrugged. "Not really. I just like plants. My mom says I have a green thumb."

"What's a green thumb?"

"It means that when you plant things, they grow."

"My grandma Po Po in Shanghai has a green thumb," I said.

At the end of the block, we turned right, and in front of us was the hill up to Sarah's house.

Sam came running down to meet us. "Hi, Tina," he said, trying to catch his breath. "You guys want to play four-square?"

"We're carving wood," Sarah said.

"After you're done?"

"We'll see," Sarah said.

"I have something for you," I said, stopping to unzip my book bag.

Sam's face was so open and his black hair stood straight up in back. I handed him the whistle. He turned it around in his hands. "Wow, you can really carve stuff."

He put his mouth around the whistle, took a deep breath, and blew hard. Out came a deep solid sound. His whole face lit up.

"Now I can whistle," he said, running up the street so he could show his mom. "Thanks, Tina. Thanks a lot." At the driveway, he turned back to us. "Do you have a brother or a sister?"

"No." I almost said "Not yet," but somehow I wasn't ready to tell anyone our secret, not even Sarah and Sam. "But you can be my Di Di."

"Di Di?"

"Little brother in Chinese."

"I'm a Di Di," he said to Sarah. Then he blew his whistle twice.

Sarah and I headed to the honeysuckle house to look at the carving book. "How about we try making the bow and arrow," Sarah suggested. "Honeysuckle's probably good for that."

We found two long branches for the bows. We took turns using the knife to whittle off the bark. Then Sarah went in to get some string while I looked around for arrows. We strung the bows pretty tight. The book said the arrows would fly straighter that way. Sarah put an arrow to the bow, pulled it back with the string, and let it fly. It hit the locust tree. We practiced shooting until we could aim for the tree and hit it most of the time.

"I bet we could really hunt with these," Sarah said, eyeing a squirrel on Victoria's roof. It went into the broken window and came back a few minutes later with two small squirrels behind it.

"Look. I think that's a mother squirrel with two babies!" I whispered.

The mother was trying to get the babies to follow her from the roof over to the locust tree, but they were afraid to jump. Finally one jumped, but the other perched on the edge of the roof and made little noises in his throat.

"He's afraid," I said.

"I don't blame him. It's a big jump," Sarah said.

Our eyes met. "I would be afraid too." I looked down. "I am afraid in America."

"Of what?"

How could I explain? I was afraid of Ching, Chang, and Chung and of the girls who made their eyes slanted and of jumping off Victoria's windowsill and of the Immigration people who might never give us the green card. "Everything."

"Me too."

I looked up quickly. "But you were born here. You're American."

"I'm still scared."

"Of what?"

Sarah was quiet for a minute. "I don't know. Lots of

stuff. Like teachers who mix up the Chinese kids."

"I know. The gym teacher keeps calling me Sarah."

"She does?"

I nodded. "But she's a nice lady. She doesn't mean to mix us up."

The mother squirrel was waiting on the tree trunk, calling to her baby. He was scurrying back and forth along the roof gutter, making louder and louder noises, but he wouldn't jump. Finally the mother and the other baby scrambled up the tree, leaving the one baby stranded.

Crouched on the top of the roof right behind the baby squirrel was the kitten, now almost as big as a cat. "Stop, stop!" I shouted.

Sarah saw him too. "No," she yelled. "Kitty, *no!*"

Sam blew his whistle. The kitten was ready to spring.

Sarah pulled the bow back and took aim. What if she hit him? Or the squirrel? The bow was strung tight. The arrow could kill a small animal. She shut one eye, steadied her arm, and let go. The arrow flew straight into the brick wall of Victoria's house. The kitten scrambled down the shingles. Then, finally, the baby squirrel made the jump.

We sat together in the honeysuckle house. The kitten came in and rolled around in the dirt. "Now he looks so peaceful. Do you think he really could kill a baby squirrel?" I asked.

Sarah stroked his short gray fur. "Maybe."

"Good thing he didn't."

Suddenly the kitten attacked my leg with his little feet, but it didn't hurt. "You aren't scared of him anymore," Sarah said.

"Not so much. I think I am used to him now."

I picked up a stick and dragged it in the dirt. The kitten gave up on my leg and jumped for the stick.

We heard a scrambling noise above us. Way up in the oak tree, the three squirrels were playing tag around the tree trunk. One of the babies jumped to the locust tree and over to Victoria's roof. The other one followed.

"I guess they got used to the jump already," I said.

Sarah nodded.

The kitten was sniffing around by my feet. Then he jumped onto my lap and curled up. Sarah smiled. "Good thing you got used to him," she said.

"And he got used to me."

"Wait here," Sarah said.

She went into her house and came back a minute later with a hairbrush. She said she would fix my hair any way I wanted it.

"One ponytail," I said.

She took out the colored rubber bands and put them on a stone. Then she brushed my hair in long strokes all the way down. "Your hair is lighter than mine."

"Like my dad's," I said.

Sarah felt her short hair. "Mine's more like my mom's."

"Were your grandparents from China?" I asked.

"Yup."

"Did you ever meet them?"

"Yup. They live in California now," Sarah said. "But all my great-uncles are still in China."

"Do you want to visit there someday?"

Sarah didn't answer right away. "I'm not sure. I don't speak Chinese."

"I can go with you," I said. "We can stay in Shanghai with my grandma Po Po. Anyway I might be living in Shanghai again if my dad doesn't get that green card."

Sarah kept brushing my hair. Then she asked, "Do you want to go back?"

In China, Uncle would teach me how to really carve. I could carve a name stamp for Sarah. Po Po would make her delicious frog soup. But in America, Ma Ma could be a nurse. Ba Ba would get a job with a big company and we could buy our small house. Suddenly I remembered our new baby. In China there could be only one child in our family. It was too crowded there already. We had to stay in America. Our baby would be born in America, our American baby. But what if they said no, no green card for you? "I don't know," I whispered.

Sarah pulled my hair back into one high ponytail just like Naomi's. "Now it's my turn to brush yours," I said.

"It's too short to do much with," Sarah said.

"I can fix it like Mu Ying's."

We switched seats so that Sarah was in front of me. I parted her hair on the side and brushed it down. Then I made a small ponytail on top. We went inside to look in the mirror. Suddenly Sarah was laughing. "Now you look like the American girl and I look like the Chinese girl," she said.

I was laughing too. Sam came in to see what was so funny. He made us both bunny ears with his fingers. Then all three of us were laughing so hard we couldn't stop. Sarah's mom took a picture of us like that with Sam in the middle blowing his whistle.

**PUBLIC SCHOOL 309**
794 MONROE STREET
BROOKLYN, NEW YORK 11221

| DATE DUE | | | |
|---|---|---|---|
| JAN 03 '06 | | | |
| MAY 17 '06 | | | |
| | | | |
| | | | |
| | | | |
| | | | |
| | | | |
| | | | |
| | | | |
| | | | |

F
CHE

Cheng, Andrea.

Honeysuckle house

PUBLIC SCHOOL 309
794 MONROE STREET
BROOKLYN, NEW YORK 11221

P.S. 309 LIBRARY
794 MONROE ST
BROOKLYN, NY 11221

410301 01440        01102C        002